PRAISE FOR *The Secret History of Us*:

"Jessi Kirby's books just keep getting better and better, and *The Secret History of Us* is her best yet. It beautifully touches on all the most important things in life— love, family, friendship, memory, and bacon. I loved it."
—Morgan Matson, *New York Times* bestselling author of *The Unexpected Everything*

PRAISE FOR *Things We Know by Heart*:

"Above all else, *Things We Know by Heart* explores the possibility of finding human connection through tragic loss. Couple that with Kirby's gift for detail and writing relatable characters and you get not just a love story but one with a ferocious pulse."
—John Corey Whaley, Printz Award–winning author of *Where Things Come Back*

"This is hands down Jessi Kirby's best book to date. It's stunning and breathtaking, at turns heartbreaking and healing."
—Sarah Ockler, author of *Twenty Boy Summer*

"The love story will hook readers—especially those who enjoyed John Green's *The Fault in Our Stars*. This memorable romance will ring true with teens."
—*SLJ*

"Well-rounded characters and the romantic tension of unrevealed secrets."
—*Kirkus Reviews*

"Kirby's story is, at its core, a sweet, budding romance, set against the backdrop of family. A story of letting go and moving forward."
—*Publishers Weekly*

"Kirby's writing is lush and emotional. . . . A satisfying romance. Like Ockler's similarly themed and similarly enjoyable *Twenty Boy Summer*, this brings all the poignancy and sentiment that a genre fan could wish."
—*BCCB*

"Kirby weaves a sweet romance in the same spirit as Susane Colasanti and Lauren Barnholdt."
—*VOYA*

"A sweet romance that grows organically."
—Unshelved.com

Also by Jessi Kirby
Golden
In Honor
Moonglass
Things We Know by Heart

THE

SECRET

HISTORY

OF *us*

JESSI KIRBY

An Imprint of HarperCollins*Publishers*

HarperTeen is an imprint of HarperCollins Publishers.

The Secret History of Us
Copyright © 2017 by Jessi Kirby
All rights reserved. Printed in the United States of America.

Library of Congress Control Number: 2016963706
ISBN 978-0-06-229946-8 (trade bdg.) — ISBN 978-0-06-267204-9 (int. ed.)

Typography by Erin Fitzsimmons
17 18 19 20 21 PC/LSCH 10 9 8 7 6 5 4 3 2 1
❖
First Edition

To the students and staff at El Rancho School—
thank you for so many fun memories!
I will cherish them always.

THE
SECRET
HISTORY
OF *us*

The girl he pulls to the surface is dead. I know it the moment I see her.

The camera zooms in, shaking a little as she comes into focus. Even in the golden lights shining down from the bridge, her skin is an unnatural shade of blue. Her top hangs loose and heavy with water from one shoulder, revealing a black bra strap. Long, dark hair streaks down her face in waves, covering her eyes, nose, mouth, and I want to brush it away so she can breathe, but the blue of her skin says it wouldn't help. She isn't breathing. She can't feel the hair covering her face or the water that moves in her lungs instead of air.

She can't feel anything.

Not the arms that drag her dead weight from the dark water, or the crack of her skull against the boat as they lift her into it. Not the hands that lay her down roughly on the deck, then feel her neck, her wrists, anywhere for a pulse. She doesn't feel the bite of the night air against her bare skin when they rip her shirt open, straight down the center, without hesitating.

I watch, relieved that she can't feel the force of those hands as they come together, one on top of the other, in the middle of her chest, and thrust downward. Deep enough to produce a contraction in her motionless heart. Hard enough to send a rush of blood and oxygen through her body, to her brain. Strong enough to crack ribs.

I wince at this, and at those hands that come down again and again, the full weight of the person behind them compressing her chest, her lifeless body convulsing under the force of them each time. Over and over.

But then, like a reprieve, the hands stop, brush the hair from her face, almost gently, and tilt her chin to the sky. The camera zooms in on her face just as he pinches her nose and brings his mouth to her blue lips. He breathes his own air into her lungs before his hands move back to the center of her chest to start the cycle again.

Her mouth begins to foam.

Sirens whine in the distance. Voices off camera murmur urgent words that are lost in the wind. Someone is crying.

"My God," the voice from behind the camera says, "it's too late. There's no way she's going to live."

ONE

"LIV?"

It's a voice that's familiar. Warm in a way the makes me want to keep hearing it. Comforting, but I can't place it. I search. Through the water or the fog—I can't tell which because it's everywhere, all around me.

But I know this voice. I know her.

Her.

I grasp at the word, reach for something to pair it with. A name . . . a face . . . something, anything, but I come up empty, except for that familiar feeling.

"We're right here, Livvy. Right here," the voice—*she*—says, and I feel a gentle hand on mine. It doesn't poke or prod, just sits there, still and warm, and I relax at the touch, and the sound of my nickname.

"Hey, Liv," another voice says gently. A male voice. "Can you hear me?" he asks.

I know this one too. And I can feel the answer, just beyond my reach. I wade through the heaviness all around me, fumble through the haze that seems endless, and this time I don't come up empty. I find the answer.

Yes, I can hear you. Yes. Yes. Yes.

"If you can hear me, sweetheart, try to open your eyes."

Sweetheart . . .

I hang on to that word he said.

Sweetheart . . .

That word he always says.

Good night, sweetheart.

I know this.

Be safe, sweetheart . . .

I know him . . .

Wake up, sweetheart.

Dad.

The word materializes from the fog crystal clear, like it's always been there, and it makes me so happy I want him to keep talking. Keep asking me questions.

"Can you wake up, Liv? Open your eyes?"

My eyes. I remember them too now and try to do what he asks, but they are weighted down—impossible, leaden things that won't be moved.

"She will," the first voice says, and I know all at once it's my mom. Her warm hand squeezes mine and I squeeze back, but she doesn't notice. "She'll wake up when she's ready."

But I'm awake. I'm here!

I try to say the words. Try to let them know that I can hear them. I need them to know that their voices are so clear, and I *know* who they are, and I want them to stay with me. I don't want them to leave me alone in this dream-fog place, with the never-ending beeping and buzzing and muffled voices of strangers, and strange hands that move me around, touching and checking me in what seems like a constant cycle. I summon every bit of strength I have to form the words, but they get lost in the haze between my brain and my mouth.

It's quiet except for the machines. I panic. I don't want them to leave me. I need to say something so they don't leave me.

I try again, harder this time, and after a moment, a tiny sound—cracked and desert-dry—comes burning from somewhere deep in my throat.

My mom's hand squeezes again, and I remember it's there. Again I squeeze back, and again she doesn't notice. *Why doesn't she notice?*

"Did you hear that?" my dad asks. "I heard something, Suze. She made a sound."

I feel the weight of his large hand come to my shoulder. "We're right here, sweetheart. Your mom and I are right here."

I try again to speak, and the cracked sound turns into a low moan that I don't recognize. It burns in my throat, and in my ears, but the harder I try to make it stop, the louder it gets.

"It's okay, baby," my mom's voice says. "*You're* okay, you're just waking up, that's all. You've had a nice long sleep, and you're waking up."

Waking up.

When she says the words, I understand that's what I need to do. That's what they want me to do. I do my best, concentrate on my eyes. Make them blink, just barely. The brightness sends a flash of pain through my head. I cry out so loud it scares me, and squeeze my eyes shut as hard as I can.

"The light, Bruce," my mom says. "Get the light."

I hear a shuffle and then the click of a switch, and in my head I try to calm down, but my skull is pounding and my throat is burning and I can't.

"Sshhh . . . it's okay," my mom says, running her warm hand over my forehead now. "It's okay."

I realize I'm still making that low, terrible sound, still squeezing my eyes closed so hard it hurts.

My dad is next to me again, his hand back on my

shoulder, his voice soft and low. "Hey, hey, hey, you don't have to wake up yet. You just wait until you feel good and ready."

The lightning strike in my head is gone, but tiny ripples of pain still radiate outward from someplace deep inside. I'm scared to open my eyes again, but I want to wake up, I do. I want to wake up and go home, and leave this place, whatever, wherever it is.

I try to relax my eyelids enough to let them flutter open, just a little, bracing for the pain to come flashing through my head again. But this time it doesn't. I open my eyes a tiny bit more, and now I can see something. I can see the blurred outlines on either side of me—my parents. And I can hear the sudden cry from my mom, and the laugh that escapes from my dad as he leans over me and kisses my forehead.

"There you are," he says.

For a few seconds, it feels like someone is turning the lights up slowly. And then it happens.

I wake up.

TWO

A YOUNG-LOOKING NURSE gazes at me. "Do you know who these two people are, Olivia?"

The question seems so ridiculous it confuses me for a second. I study my mom, and then my dad, trying to figure out what I could possibly be missing. They both look tired—the lines on their faces are deeper than I've ever seen. My mom's roots are growing out, and my dad's hair looks like it's thinned overnight. Even so—they are, without a doubt, my parents. I look back at the nurse.

"My . . . mom and dad?" My voice comes out unsure. An answer like a question.

"She knew us right away," my mom says, stepping closer

and grabbing my hand again. "As soon as she woke up. That's a good sign, right?"

The nurse nods. "Yes, it is. Everything about today is a good sign. That she woke up so quickly once we turned the meds down, that she knew you right away . . ."

I glance at my parents. That I *knew* them right away? I don't understand.

The nurse pauses and turns to me. Smiles like she knows me. "It's so good to finally meet you, Olivia. I'm Betina. I've been helping to take care of you here."

My name sounds strange when she says it, and I'm not sure how to answer, so I don't.

This doesn't seem to bother her, and she turns, addressing my parents instead. "She's got grit, this one. No doubt. Dr. Tate is in an emergency surgery right now, but as soon as she's finished, she'll be up to check on you, and tomorrow we'll do a full assessment. In the meantime . . ."

She pauses and looks back at me with warm brown eyes. "You just take it easy, sweetie. You made it through the hard part, and you're here, and awake, and that is all you need to be right now, you got that?"

I nod, wondering what else I would do, and why she's been taking care of me, but I don't want to ask any of these things in front of her, so I keep quiet. She smiles at me before looking back at my parents. "Have *you two* got that?"

It's more like a command than a question, punctuated with a raised eyebrow and a stern look. "Just be here with her."

My mom—and even my dad—both nod obediently, like this woman who looks too young to be a nurse is the boss of them. It makes me worry, the way they seem so nervous. They seem to need her reassurance, like I'm a broken, fragile thing.

I try to sit up a little taller to show them I'm neither, but a shock of pain zips around my chest when I move. I wince. Lie back down.

"Olivia," Betina says, in a firm mom-tone, "I mean it when I say take it easy. You have a lot of healing to do yet."

I bring my hand to the center of my chest. "It hurts . . ." I can't finish. Can't tell her that it hurts to move or breathe, because my throat feels too bruised and raw to say so.

She nods. "You have four broken ribs. If the pain gets to be too much, just let me know, and we can give you something more for it."

I move my hand from my chest up to my throat, hoping she'll understand that I mean to ask about the burning ache there. She nods again. "You had a breathing tube, so it's going to feel like you've got a bad case of strep throat for a day or two. But don't worry," she says. "Mouths heal quickly, and pretty soon you'll be right back to eating normally."

I vaguely wonder what I'll eat until then, but I don't

have the energy to ask. I nod, careful not to move anything besides my head. I don't know what else may be wrong with me, and I don't want any more painful surprises.

Betina turns back to my parents.

"And let's keep the good news to just family and close friends right now. Soon as those media people hear about it, they'll be circling right back around here like vultures, and that's the last thing she needs is to have—"

"Of course," my mom says quickly.

"Media?" I rasp. But no one answers me.

My mom follows Betina across the room, to the doorway. She glances at me, then lowers her voice, but not quite enough. I can still hear her when she says, "What if she asks . . . what do we—I just don't want to overwhelm her with everything that's happened . . ."

Betina looks my way and, when she sees I'm listening, doesn't match my mom's lowered voice. "Then don't. But answer her questions, Mrs. Jordan. She's been through a lot, but your daughter is a strong young woman." Now she looks back at me. "You remember that, Olivia. You are strong. A fighter. You've already shown us all that."

I'm not sure if it's the familiar way she speaks to me, or her words, or my parents' emotion and obvious trust in her, but it makes me feel good when she says this, despite the growing worry and confusion in my head.

"Liv," I say, surprising all of us. My voice sounds as raw as my throat feels. "My friends call me Liv." My throat aches, but a complete sentence feels like an accomplishment.

"Liv. Now that doesn't surprise me one bit."

A smile spreads over her face and lingers in her eyes a moment before she turns on one white-sneakered heel and is gone. I am left in the hospital room with the slow, steady beeping of the monitors on one side of my bed, and my mom and dad on the other. They both smile at me, but their smiles are more tentative than the nurse's was, like they're not sure what comes next.

Which makes three of us.

We're all quiet, and I look around the room, taking in the bright bouquets of flowers that burst from the vases that cover every available surface in the room. Shiny bunches of balloons hover in the corners, and a stuffed bear bigger than me props up a Get Well Soon sign that's thick with handwriting in all different shades of markers. Cards and posters cover the wall facing me. This can't all be for me. I don't even know that many people.

"You didn't know you were so popular, did you?" my dad says with a laugh.

"So many people have been so kind and thoughtful," my mom adds.

I feel like I'm in a dream. Or watching a movie.

The sun slants soft through the blinds, and I can feel them watching me, waiting for me to say something, or to ask something. There are a thousand questions running through my mind, swirling around unformed, bumping into each other, needing to be answered, but the simplest one is the one I finally ask out loud, in a voice that doesn't quite sound like my own.

"What . . ." I pause, not entirely sure I want to know the answer. "What *happened*?"

They both take in a deep breath at the same time. Exchange a glance like they're deciding who will be the one to answer me. My mom looks from me to my dad and back again. He clears his throat.

"You were in an accident, sweetheart."

"What . . ." I try to ignore the pain in my throat and the tremor in my voice. "What accident? Why am I . . ."

I look down at myself—at the bracelet with my name printed on it around my wrist, the tubes and wires taped to the inside of my arms. The gown that hides my broken ribs and who knows what else on this body that doesn't even feel like mine.

"What happened to me?" I ask again, but now my voice is almost a whisper.

My mom presses her lips together, steps toward the bed, and takes my hand in both of hers. Her bottom lip quivers, and she bites it, her eyes welling up. It feels like my fault that she's crying.

"I'm sorry," I say. "I'm sorry . . ." Now it's me who's

blinking back tears, because it doesn't seem like I should have to ask her that question. I should know the answer because it's *me*, lying here. How could I not know what happened to my own body? I search my brain for some feeling or clue, but there's only a heavy absence. The static hiss of nothing.

My dad wraps his big hand around mine and pauses, looking almost sorry for what he's about to say. "You were in a car accident, Liv." His voice is calm, even, like always. It doesn't match the emotion in his eyes. He clears his throat and glances at my mom, who wipes at her cheek. "You were hit by another driver on the Carson Bridge, and your car went over—"

"My car?"

I feel like I'm playing catch-up, trying to fit his words into a story that makes sense, but none of them feel like they belong to me, and I know I'm missing something, because I don't have a car.

"The Toyota," he says, like I should know what he's talking about. "It went over, and into the bay. In fact it's still—"

"Bruce," my mom interrupts. *Stop*, her eyes tell him.

He nods, just barely. Takes a deep breath, and smiles a weary-looking smile at me. "Anyway. It was pretty serious, kiddo. They had to keep you asleep for a little while to give your body some time to rest."

"Asleep? Like a *coma*?"

My mom looks startled by the word.

"Not a coma," my dad says. "More like what they do when they perform surgery. So you wouldn't feel any pain." He pauses, glancing at my mom, whose fist is balled up in front of her mouth. Then he looks back at me. "You aspirated a lot of water that had to be suctioned out of your lungs, so they put a breathing tube in to give them time to heal."

I feel the sudden need to take a deep breath, but I don't dare, for the pain. "How long?" I ask.

I'm scared of the answer. The way they're acting seems like it must've been months. The way they look, it seems like it could be years.

"Eight days," my dad says, and I feel the tiniest bit of relief, even though this seems to set off more tears from my mom.

"We've been here every day," she says.

Dad reaches out his hand for hers, and when she takes it, he pulls her in to his side, wrapping his arm around her shoulders. "It was scary, but we knew you were gonna be okay, didn't we?"

"Yes, we did," my mom says, her voice thick with tears.

She's so upset, I'm not sure I believe her. And then it hits me. My stomach drops. "Where's Sam? Was he driving?"

I see a look pass between my parents. "No," my dad answers slowly. "Your brother's on his way back from his backpacking trip. We couldn't reach him for a few days after the accident, and when we finally did, he was still pretty far out. He's been making his way back as fast as he can."

Relief washes over me, and I'm about to go back to asking about the car again, and who was driving, and what exactly happened, but there's a voice, muffled at first, coming from the hallway. It gets louder and closer, and I recognize it as the nurse, Betina.

"I told you, miss, you are *not* allowed in this wing. I don't care what news channel you work for, this is a hospital and she is a *patient*, and security is on their way right now to remove you."

"I just need a few minutes," another female voice says. "Even with just her parents. One parent—or *you* could give me an update."

"Absolutely not," Betina says.

"But people are worried. They want to know how she's doing. There is *national* interest in this story—"

My dad is up from his chair and across the room before she can say anything else. My mom squeezes my hand, then stands and moves between my bed and the doorway, shielding me from who, or what, I have no idea.

"Who's that?" I ask. I try again to sit up straighter, crane my neck a little to see, but the pain forces me right back down. I try to breathe it away, but that hurts too.

"It's no one," my mom says over her shoulder, like I can't

see or hear that there *is* someone.

My dad stands squarely in the doorway, his wide shoulders blocking it. "You need to leave now," he says in the practiced calm that I've always thought of as his police officer voice.

There is the sound of boots in the hallway, radios.

"Officer Jordan, please. Just a few questions," the woman says. Or girl. She sounds young. And desperate. "She's awake, right? What's her condition? Is she speaking? Coherent?" There's a shuffle, muffled voices. Something falls to the floor. And then I hear her voice again, farther away now, like she's being led down the hall. "Does she know what a miracle she—"

A door slams, and I don't hear the rest of the question.

My parents look at each other before they turn to me, their eyes wide with concern, and something else I don't recognize.

A lump rises in my throat, and I feel my eyes well up again. I am so confused. I feel like I'm watching someone else's life, or like I'm in a bad dream, or . . . I can't even put it into a clear thought, because there's just this awful heavy emptiness when I try.

"Please," I whisper. "Tell me what's going on."

THREE

LATER. I DON'T know how much. But my room is still, and I am alone.

It takes a moment for my eyes to adjust to the darkness when I wake, and then a few more after that for me to remember where I am and why I'm here.

Hospital, accident, trauma . . .

I run through the words in my mind. Try to use them to ground me here, now. They still don't sound like words that belong to me. I move to sit up, but the stab of pain in my core stops me. Broken ribs. Those belong to me. Those are too real.

I reach for the call button like the nurse showed me to do if I hurt too much, but my fingers hover in the air above it, trembling. I close my eyes and wait for the pain to subside, try to keep my breaths shallow and fight through it. I don't want the dull, drowsy feeling the medication brings as it replaces the pain. Actually, I almost don't want the pain to go away. I almost need to feel it to remind me that this is real, and that something happened to me. Something I can't remember and still don't know all the details of.

I hadn't gotten a chance to ask any more questions, because the nurse came in with a list of things for me to do: swallow some water, keep it down, get out of bed. Move. Walk. At first I thought it was funny how she'd made it sound like she was asking a lot of me, and how nervous it'd made my parents. Like doing those things would be a big deal.

Then I tried the first thing on her list—to drink some water. And I understood.

Little things become big things when your body has been broken. And the big things are a struggle. Like the physical act of swallowing a tiny sip of water after having a ventilator tube in your throat for days. Or fighting the immediate wave of nausea it sets off. Or lowering your feet to the floor and trusting that somehow your legs will still be able to hold you up.

I'd done these things, and my parents had watched, murmuring words of encouragement. When I'd swallowed the water, and kept it down, they'd looked relieved. When I'd gotten out of bed, stood on shaky legs, and taken a few steps to the bathroom with their help, they'd all congratulated me like I was crossing a finish line. It had taken everything out of me—more than I'd realized it would, but they told me over and over how strong I was, and I'd tried my best to believe them.

Here, now, alone in the dark, I want to try to do more. I tell myself I'm strong, and that there are things I need to know. I tell my brain that maybe it doesn't need to protect me so much from all those things. That it's okay for me to remember the details of what happened. That I *need* to remember them, because I don't feel like myself right now.

I close my eyes and concentrate. Wait for something, anything to come to me, but my mind is as dark as the night sky. I scan the darkness, wait another moment. Hope for an image to streak across it like a shooting star, but there's nothing. Not even a pinpoint of light.

It's the loneliest thing I've ever felt.

I'm on my own for this. Alone inside myself. Across the room, a shiny balloon sways in the artificial breeze beneath a vent in the ceiling. My eyes follow the ribbon down to the table, where it's anchored. It's covered with bouquets of flowers with their tiny notes stuck into them, cards propped up in the spaces between their vases. Get Well wishes for me from people who know more about what happened to me than I do.

I move slowly this time, anticipating the pain that will come with what I'm going to do. I tell myself I can do this, and acknowledge the pain in my rib cage—my new companion everywhere I go. After a moment, I'm sitting upright. A little thing that's now a big thing. Next, I slide my legs to the edge of the bed, like Betina showed me, and carefully lower them, inch by inch, until my toes brush the floor. When they do, I'm glad for the grippy socks she'd put on my feet—lifesaving socks, she'd called them with a laugh. The floor shines slick in the light from the hall, and now that I have to do this without her help, I think I understand what she meant. It makes me nervous.

I test my weight, first on one foot, then the other, and once both feet are pressed flat to the ground, rubber pads sticking to the floor, I edge myself off the bed. The IV pole has to come with me, so I loop the tubes over my arm like she showed me. With one hand on the stand and the other trailing on the bed for balance, I move toward the end of the bed, where I'll have to let go for a moment to cross the small distance to the table that holds flowers and stuffed animals and balloons and Get Well cards.

At the end of the bed, I take a breath—not too deep— before I let go and step away. My ribs and the muscles around them protest against the extra work it takes them to help me walk the three steps to the table. I have to rest a moment when I reach it, but it's a proud moment.

I made it. And somewhere, in the flowers and cards in front of me, there will be something that helps me remember. I look at the bright bouquet of pink and white roses directly in front of me and take the little card from its plastic spear.

Dear Olivia and Jordan family,
Our thoughts and prayers are with you for a full recovery.
Please let us know if you need anything at all. We're just a
doorstep away.
All our love,
Carol and Roger

I smile. The Abifadels. They've always been my favorite neighbors because they're like grandparents to everyone on our cul-de-sac. Everyone calls them Mr. and Mrs. A for short. She always has a treat and a joke for whatever kids are around, and he cooks for an army every Sunday—all sorts of Middle Eastern dishes—then sends them around to all the neighbors. I look around, half expecting to see some gift of food from them too, and then I remember that I've been on a feeding tube for over a week. They probably knew that, and I bet they've been trying to feed my parents instead.

I glance at another bouquet; this one is a huge bunch of

some happy red flowers whose name I don't know. I pluck the card that's tucked down among them. The writing is messy, and I don't recognize it.

Liv,
Your favorites, for when you wake up.
Love you

I turn the card over, but there's no signature. I look at the red flowers again, and the words stick in my head. My favorites? I'm not even sure I have a favorite flower, but this person seems to think so. I look from the flowers to the card, and back again, hoping for some spark of recognition. The *Love you* makes it seem like I should know, but nothing comes. I give the flowers one last glance, then put the card back carefully and decide to come back to it.

I move to the next flower arrangement, which Betina had brought in earlier in the evening. It's a huge mixed bouquet with a big bunch of shiny balloons attached, and an unopened envelope. I say a silent thank-you to her for allowing me the privilege of opening it myself, now that I'm awake. Inside the envelope is not a card, but a note card, with the letters of our local news station printed across the top. I feel the pinch of my inhale in my ribs as I pull it out and read:

Dear Olivia,

*We here at KBSY are so very happy to hear you're awake—
as are many people all across the country! Since your story
broke, people have been following with great interest, and cards
and well-wishes continue to pour in. I thought you should
know just how many people care about your recovery, so I've
packaged them all up and will be sending them along soon.
In the meantime, we all wish you a speedy recovery. I hope
that when you're well, you'll help me bring your miraculous
story to all the wonderfully caring people who have been
following along. I've already spoken to Matt and Walker about
interviewing the three of you, and they seemed open to it, so
please contact me once you're on the mend!*

Sincerely,

Dana Whitmore

KBSY6

Action News

I stare at the card. At the loopy handwriting, and the
words, and the phone number written at the bottom. And
then I read it over, once, twice, three times, trying to pull
meaning from words and names I don't have any reference
for. Since my story broke? People all over the country?
Matt and Walker?

A cold knot of fear coils in my stomach, and I feel dizzy.

Sick, and lost, and like I want to cry because apparently the whole world knows what happened to me, and I still have no idea. How could my parents not have told me everything? What else don't I know? What else are they protecting me from?

I start to put the card back in its stand, and something else catches my eye. It's a few more steps to the brown leather bag that's sitting at the end of the table, but I'm so happy to see it there, I pad over without even thinking. Pain spirals through my center, and when I get to my camera bag, I force myself to be still a moment and breathe until the pain subsides enough for me to open up the bag. When I see my camera nestled there, safe and sound, it sets off a wave of tears that comes from out of nowhere. I steady myself with one hand as tears roll hot down my cheeks, and I realize I'm relieved at seeing something I recognize, something I know is mine. I hadn't thought about my camera when they'd told me about the accident, but seeing it makes me so grateful that it wasn't in the car with me. I silently thank my mom, or dad, or whoever it was who thought to bring it to me here.

I reach to lift it out of the case, just to feel the familiar weight of it in my hands, but a flash of movement draws my attention. It's in the mirror, just beyond the bathroom door. The mirror I've forgotten about until just now. Earlier, when Betina had helped me to the bathroom, I'd noticed it was there, behind her. I'd even wondered if she'd purposely put herself in front of it to protect me from seeing something I wasn't ready for.

Part of me had wanted to ask if I could look at myself, but I'd felt embarrassed, like there were bigger things I should be worrying about. Plus, I wasn't sure I could handle what I might see, so I'd kept quiet about it. Promised myself I'd look later, once everyone had gone and I could be alone.

And now I am.

I'm scared, but there's no way I can *not* look. I take a shallow breath and inch my way toward the bathroom, just until I can see someone looking back at me.

I gasp. The mirror doesn't protect me from anything.

Even in the dim light of my room, the cold, hard square of glass thrusts me into a reality I'm not ready for.

My face is battered, bruised in shades ranging from deep purple to sickly yellowish green. My lips are cracked and dry, my mouth split at the corners. Someone has braided my hair, which might have been pretty at some point, but the dull brown hair is too matted down to tell. I reach up, run my hands over it, and find the shock of a bare spot, hair growing back over stitches in spikes, unfamiliar and foreign. I look at my eyes, search for some familiarity there, but the eyes that look back at me are so watery and swollen, they look years older than they should.

The girl in the mirror blinks when I blink. She brings her hand to her face when I do. She even shakes her head at the same time I do.

But I don't know this girl in the mirror. I don't know her at all.

FOUR

IT'S LIGHT WHEN I wake again. I lie there on my back, staring at the ceiling tiles, and run through the list of words that make up my new reality. *Accident, coma, trauma . . .*

Now that I've seen what I look like, I add *broken, bruised—unrecognizable.*

There's a soft knock on the door, and when I turn my head, I see a new face. It belongs to a girl dressed in bright pink scrubs, even younger-looking than Betina.

"You're awake," she says with a bright smile. She comes in carrying a bouquet of flowers.

I move to sit up, but the pain in my ribs stops me short. I wince.

"Oh no," she says, setting the things down on my bedside

table, "let me help you with that." She grabs the bed control and pushes the button to raise the head end. I brace myself as she brings me slowly to a reclined position.

"Are you okay like this?" she asks.

I look at her and think for a second about telling her that nothing about me is okay, but her smile is so kind that I just nod.

"Thank you."

"Of course," she says. "I'm Lauren."

"Are you the daytime nurse?"

"One day, I hope. Right now I'm a hospital volunteer." She smiles again. Motions at the flowers. "These came for you this morning. Aren't they pretty?"

I look at the sunflowers in their mason jar vase. "They are." My throat feels a little better today, but I'm not much in the mood to make small talk.

It's quiet a moment.

"Your mom's here, by the way. She's down the hall talking to the nurse, but she should be right in."

"Thank you," I say, hoping that's all, and that she'll leave.

But she lingers a moment, looking almost shy. "I, um, I just wanted to say that it's pretty incredible, how strong you are. I mean, I saw what happened, and it was—"

"You were there?" Suddenly I do want to talk to her.

She looks startled. "Oh. No, I mean I saw the video of—"

"Good *morning,* sweet girl," my mom singsongs as she

comes through the doorway. She walks over to the bed and gives me a kiss on the forehead, and before I have a chance to ask Lauren what video she was talking about, she's disappeared out the doorway.

I look at my mom. "Was there a video of my accident?"

The smile tumbles from her face and she blinks twice before answering. "That's not something you—" She stops, her eyes darting out the window.

"You have *got* to be kidding me."

Something out there has caught her eye. She goes over to the window, presses her lips together, and sighs at whatever is out there, then takes out her phone and punches the screen.

"Bruce?" she says, almost immediately. "That woman is here again, parked outside with her van and camera crew." There's a pause. "No. I haven't seen her come in." She looks at me. "Liv, honey? Has anyone come in to try and talk to you this morning?"

I shake my head.

"No," she says into the phone. "Okay. Thank you. Love you." She hangs up.

"Who's out there?" I strain a little to try to see past her. I wonder if it's the same reporter from yesterday. Dana Whitmore, maybe?

"No one you need to worry about right now," my mom

says. "Your dad's taking care of it." She turns and looks out the window again, and twists the blinds closed. Tight.

Then she turns to me, smooths her face into a smile, and comes back to my bedside. "I'm sorry," she says. "That's not how I meant to come in. Let's start over again." She takes a deep breath and lets it out slowly. Runs a soft hand over my forehead. "How are you feeling?"

I look at my mom. Really look at her, for the first time since I've woken up. She's wearing a tank top and khaki shorts—her standard teacher-on-summer-break uniform. She looks tired. There are bags under her eyes, and more lines at the corners of them than I've ever seen. I feel a twinge of guilt knowing that she probably hasn't slept a full night since the accident, and it's enough to make me set aside my questions for now. She needs a simple answer.

"Better," I say. It's partly true.

She brightens. "The nurses said you made it through the night without any painkillers. That's a good sign. Your ribs must not be hurting you too much then? That's such great progress, sweetheart." She glances at the sunflowers on the bedside table, then at the shelf opposite.

"Oh, wow, look at that!" she says. "Those are just beautiful!" She walks over and examines the giant bouquet from KBSY, pushing the flowers gently to each side. I know what she's looking for. "No card? That's strange. Who would send such a beautiful arrangement without including at least a quick note? Or maybe it got lost? I wonder if we could find out from the florist?"

She's nervous. This is what my mom does when she's nervous. She just keeps talking. And maybe now she thinks if she just keeps talking about the flowers, I won't ask any more questions about the news van outside, or the video, or anything else.

I think of the note card I'd tucked safely under my pillow last night and I almost mention it. But something holds me back. "I don't know," I say instead.

She glances at the flowers again, and then looks back at me. "Anyway. I have a surprise for you, if you're feeling up to it."

I'm not sure I'm feeling up to any surprises right now, but she has this little hopeful smile, and I don't want to hurt her feelings. "What is it?"

"It's not a what, it's a who. Dr. Tate said now that you're stable, it would be all right. That it'd probably even be good for you to have some visitors."

"Is Sam here?" The thought of seeing my brother actually lifts my spirits a little. He'd crack some jokes. Make me feel normal. Tell me what happened if I could get him alone.

My mom tilts her head and smiles like she's surprised. "No, he'll be home tomorrow. He's on his way back from the trailhead in the Eastern Sierras, remember?" Her phone chimes, and she looks down at the screen, then taps a quick answer.

"Oh, perfect," she says. "That's Paige. She just got here, if you want to see her." She stops. Frowns. "I'm sorry. I should've asked you first. Is that okay?"

"Of course!" I sit up and look toward the hallway, mostly ignoring the pain that comes with the movement. "Yes! Yes, I want to see her. Is Jules here too?"

My mom frowns. "No, you two haven't—" She bites her lip. "It's just Paige for now. Poor thing's been so worried about you, but I didn't want her to see you like—until you woke up. I'll go get her right now."

She disappears out the doorway, and I sit there, trying to figure out what she started to say about Jules, and why she wouldn't be here with Paige. A few moments later, I hear footsteps, and a voice I recognize, coming down the hallway. Paige's voice. "I hope it's okay, Mrs. Jordan. I just knew she'd want to see him too."

"I don't have to go in right now, if it's too much," a male voice says.

The footsteps stop outside the doorway.

"It's all right, honey," my mom answers. "You just surprised me, that's all. I'm sure she'll be happy to see you both." She lowers her voice now, enough that I can hear her whisper-talking but can't make out the words. I'm straining to hear, and trying to figure out who Paige brought with her, and all of a sudden I feel anxious. This keeps happening. Everyone keeps doing and saying things faster than I can follow, and I feel like I'm two steps behind, and it almost makes me want to cry. But I can't, because right then, they all come in.

For a moment, it's silent.

And then I can hear the intake of their breath—of Paige and the boy who hangs back in the doorway.

"It's okay," I hear my mom say. "She's okay. Come on in."

I can't do anything but stare, because the girl who steps forward looks like Paige but doesn't at the same time.

She's taller and curvier, with shiny blond hair that's straight instead of curly, bright white teeth with no braces, and brows arched over eyes that wear more makeup than Paige is allowed to.

As soon as we make eye contact, tears spill down her cheeks, and she's immediately at my bedside, both of her hands wrapped around mine. "Oh my God, Liv," she says, "you're really okay."

I don't know what to say. I just look at her, trying to get my bearings with this version of Paige. Her eyes run over me like she's doing the same, and I flash on the image of my reflection in the mirror last night. If it scares her as much as it did me, she doesn't let it show.

She squeezes my hands. "You're a miracle," she says,

looking right into my eyes. Her mascara is running, and she sniffs, then dabs at her nose. "I'm sorry. I know I shouldn't cry. But I've been a total mess—so worried. I don't know what I would've done if . . . if . . ." She shakes her head and dabs at her nose again. Sits up straighter. "Anyway. I just love you so much, and I'm so thankful you're okay, and . . ."

She trails off, and it's quiet, and I know I should say something. She needs me to say something.

"I love you too," I say softly.

This sets off a whole new wave of tears in Paige, and she leans in and gives me a gentle hug. Over her shoulder, I can see my mom fighting off her own tears, and the boy standing in the doorway like he's afraid to come in, and really I don't blame him with all this going on.

Our eyes meet and he looks down at the floor.

Paige releases me from the hug and I look at her. "Where's Jules?"

She gives me a strange look. "I don't know. We don't . . . She's not . . ."

She looks to my mom for help, but a nurse I don't recognize steps into the room. "Mrs. Jordan?"

"Yes?"

"Dr. Tate would like a word with you now, if that's okay."

"Oh. I . . ." My mom looks at me. "Are you okay if I step out for a minute, sweetheart?"

Paige smiles at me. "We'll keep her company."

"Okay?" my mom asks again.

I nod.

"Hopefully I won't be long," she says. And she turns to follow the nurse back out into the hallway. When she gets to the boy, she puts a hand on his shoulder. "It's okay," she says, and then she lets her hand fall as she steps past him into the hallway.

This seems to be what he was waiting for, and he takes a step fully into the room. He's tall and athletic-looking in sweats and a T-shirt. Handsome. One of his arms is in a sling; his opposite hand, bandaged. There are bruises beneath his eyes—bruises like I saw in the mirror last night.

I can feel Paige watching me as I try desperately to add up all the details.

"I'm sorry," she says. She looks from me, over her shoulder, at the boy. "I know you two probably have a lot to talk about, I can go—"

"No," I say, more forcefully than I mean to. "Stay. Please." I hold on to her hand. Tight.

She glances at the boy, then nods at me. "Okay. I'll stay."

It's quiet.

"Liv," he says finally, and I startle at the sound of my nickname and the tremor in his voice when he says it. Like he knows me. Like I should know him.

His bandaged hand shakes the slightest bit as he takes a few steps toward the bed.

"I'm so sorry," he says.

I tighten my grip on Paige's hand, and try to ignore the rawness of his voice and the worry it triggers in my chest: that something is very, very wrong. I should know who he is. I should know what he's sorry about.

"God, I'm sorry. I don't even know what to—I didn't know what hit us. We went over so fast, and then we hit the water, and it came pouring through the windows, and the airbags were everywhere—I couldn't see anything."

His words sink in—*we . . . us . . .*

The accident.

"You were in the accident too?"

I look at him, and all of a sudden it feels hard to breathe.

"I couldn't find you at first," he says. "I got out, and I dove back down, over and over." He shakes his head. "And then I did find you, but I . . ." He looks at me now. "You were stuck and I couldn't get you out." He runs his hands over his face and through his hair, and looks at me with glassy eyes. "I'm so sorry, Liv."

My throat tightens, and I try to take a breath, but it hurts. I look at Paige, beg her silently to tell me what's going on.

She just squeezes my hand.

"Liv?" His eyes plead with me. "Say something. Please."

"I don't . . ."

Worry creases his forehead. "I know you don't remember. I just . . . wanted you to know that I tried. I would've traded my life for yours if I could have." He takes a step closer and reaches out a tentative hand. Rests it on the edge of the bed. "I love you, Liv."

I press my lips together and try to keep from crying, but it's too late and there's no other way to say what I need to.

"I'm sorry," I say. "But I don't . . ."

I can hardly bring myself to say it, because of the look on his face, and because now I'm certain something is very, very wrong.

My voice is shaky and hollow when I finally form the words.

"I don't know you."

Confusion spreads over his face. "What do you mean?"

I glance at Paige, who seems just as worried and confused as he is. "Liv?" She looks from me to him and back again, alarm in her eyes. "Liv, what's wrong? What's going on? It's *Matt*."

I look back at the boy standing there by the bed, and I repeat the only thing I know to be true in this moment.

"I don't know who you are."

FIVE

DR. TATE STANDS next to my bed, and my parents hover at the end of it. My dad is in his uniform—he came straight from work when my mom called him. She'd come back to the room to find Paige still holding my hand, Matt pacing quietly, and me sitting there feeling like I'd failed them both terribly.

They'd gone silent when I'd finally said I didn't know who he was, looked at each other in that worried way people have been doing around me, hoping I don't notice, since I woke up. It was a relief for all of us when my mom had come in. I think even more so for them when, after we told her everything, she thanked them for coming, suggested that I needed some rest so they should probably go, hugged them both, and assured them that she'd call later with an update. As soon as they walked out the door, she called the nurse on duty, who called Dr. Tate.

That was hours ago.

Since then, Dr. Tate has taken me through a series of tests that started with questions like what was my full name, and when was my birthday. After I got those questions right, we'd moved on to me counting backward and repeating sequences of words, identifying the names of everyday objects in pictures, and answering questions like whether or not a stone floats on water.

It had all felt strange and ridiculous, but those were all tests I had passed. It was the questions that came after, the ones my parents had asked me, that I didn't have the answers for. Questions about Matt, and school, and volleyball. Birthdays, and dances, and summers spent working at the marina. They'd gone backward in time with their questions, starting from this morning when I didn't know who Matt was, until finally we got to the summer before freshman year, and I started to have some answers.

Which brings us here, now.

Dr. Tate flips through the last few pages on my chart, then closes it in her hands and focuses all her attention on us. "Based on the full CAP assessment, and the questions you've helped me ask her, I believe Liv is experiencing posttraumatic retrograde amnesia." She looks at me now.

"You've been through a major trauma—one in which you were without oxygen for an extended period of time." She turns to my parents. "That could be the cause, or it could be the blow she suffered to the head when she was pulled onto the boat. In either case, based on the memories she is able to recall, we know she's missing a period of recent years." She looks back at me. "Between four and five, as far as we can tell. Right?"

I close my eyes, try to wrap my mind around what Dr. Tate is saying.

That I died for a few moments and came back missing years of my life. That there are years of the life I've lived that I do not remember. Years that still feel like they're ahead of me. Days I was looking forward to. Big moments I've already had. They're gone. Like they were never mine.

"What does this mean? Is it permanent?" my mom asks.

It's quiet for a long moment, and I open my eyes and look at Dr. Tate, who's looking at me.

"It's hard to say. In many of these cases, some or all of a person's memories return over time. In others, they don't. At this point, it's a waiting game."

"So we just have to wait and *see*?" My mom's voice is shaky now.

Dr. Tate nods sympathetically. "I know that's not the answer you want, but as hard as that sounds, yes. We'll continue to assess her and monitor any progress we see, but there's very little we can do for this besides give it time."

Now my dad chimes in. "There has to be something we can we do to help her—besides wait and see. That doesn't—there's got to be something more."

Dr. Tate nods, like she understands. "You can take her home. Get her back to her routines, and the things she's used to doing. Surround her with the familiar."

"She can come home? When?" my mom asks, like she doesn't believe it. Then her brows furrow. "Are you sure? That seems awfully fast, especially with her . . . with this."

"She's made it through the most critical part of her recovery, is stable, and healing. Our job is to get her back to her life now. I'd like to keep her here tonight, but tomorrow morning you can bring her home," Dr. Tate says.

She looks at all of us and smiles, like that should be great news.

My mom takes a deep breath and nods like she's telling herself that it'll be okay. My dad comes to the head of my bed and puts his hand on my shoulder and squeezes. I sit there, terrified. I don't know what my life even is. I don't know what it looks like now. I want to go home to my own room, and bed, and things, but I don't know if I'll even recognize them as mine. I don't know what will be there, and what will be missing.

So far, I've found out it's a lot.

I know my family, and my little beach town. I have fond

and not-so-fond memories of being a kid. I remember Sydney, our golden retriever, and how much I loved her, and how sad I was when we had to put her to sleep. I remember the bike I got for my tenth birthday, and the day I fell off it and broke my arm. I remember slumber parties and family vacations. My best friends and my first kiss. I remember who I was. But all those memories are just the edge pieces of the puzzle.

I'm missing the pieces that make up the picture in the middle. The pieces of who I am now.

Today I learned that I'm eighteen years old, but the last birthday I can remember celebrating is my fourteenth. I graduated high school a month ago, but I've never been. I've stopped hanging out with one of my best friends in the whole world and I have no idea why. And I have a boyfriend—Matt—who I'm head over heels in love with, but who I only just met today. He's a victim of the accident in more ways than one. A stranger.

Or maybe I'm the stranger. That's what it feels like, and it makes me afraid—that I won't know how to go home. Or know what to do when I get there. That I won't know how to be me.

"Well, that's great news," my dad says.

Dr. Tate nods. "We'll continue to monitor her progress. I've already booked her first appointment with our neuropsychologist. She'll need to continue her course of antibiotics to rule out any infections, and we'll send you home with some pain medication, though judging by last night and today, I don't think she'll need it." She looks at me now. "Of course, you'll need to take it easy for a while. Listen to what your body's telling you, pain-wise. It's okay to walk around, but those ribs will be sore for some time, so take it slow. For the next few weeks, you may be more tired than usual, so rest. Okay?"

I just nod, as I try to take in what she's telling me. The only thing I can think is that I don't know what my usual is. And that somehow, they think it's okay for me to go home like this.

SIX

DISCHARGE DAY. AFTER I've demonstrated that I can swallow breakfast, which is a few spoonfuls of oatmeal, and my vitals have all been checked for the last time, my IVs are removed, my bracelets are cut off, and I'm given the change of clothes my mom has brought for me.

I still don't believe they're going to let me go home, even as she helps me dress. We move slowly, carefully, because even small movements send pain radiating through my rib cage. I watch in the mirror as she sweeps my hair up into a messy bun, since I can't raise my arms over my head to do it myself.

"Your hair is so thick," she says, struggling with the

rubber band. It snaps, and my dirty hair falls back over my shoulders. I stare at the long tangles. Start to cry.

"Oh, honey," she says, meeting my eyes in the mirror. "Don't cry. It's okay. I don't know why I was trying to put it up. You always wear it down, anyway."

"I do?" I ask her, trying to hold back more tears. I don't even know this about myself anymore.

"Yeah." She seems to consider the question for a moment. "Well, let's see. You put it up for volleyball, of course. And when you're doing your homework. And at night after you've washed your face." She smiles at me now. "But when you go to school, or out with Matt, or anywhere else, you wear it long and loose, and it's beautiful that way."

I stare at my reflection, trying to picture it. Trying to see past the oily hair and bruises to the me she's talking about, but I can't see her there.

"Tell you what. Later tonight, if you're feeling up to it, I'll wash your hair for you, and you can see for yourself. How's that?"

I nod. "Okay."

"Good. For now, let's just get you home."

At the nurse's station, she fills out the last of the paperwork for me to be officially discharged, and when I see my dad pull up outside, I'm relieved that it's in our old Suburban that I remember. He gets out and helps me into the front seat, clicks the seat belt over me, and then pauses before he closes the door.

"My girl," he says, and his eyes start to well up. He smiles and shakes it off. "I'm so glad you're okay."

"Me too," I answer, though I don't feel like I am.

He closes the door gently, and my mom puts a hand on my shoulder from where she shares the backseat with all the flowers and cards from my room. I breathe in as deep as my chest will allow, and we pull out of the hospital parking lot and head home on a road I remember, through the town I've lived in my entire life.

"You okay?" my mom asks.

I am standing in the doorway of my bedroom. "Yeah." I nod. "I'm okay." I'm trying to be, at least. I can feel her watching me take it in.

"Anything coming back? Now that we're home?"

I shake my head.

Her eyes run over me, and then the room. "It looks different than you remember, doesn't it?"

I nod. It does and doesn't look like the room I remember.

"That's because we redid it two years ago. Before you started your junior year. You'd been asking for a while, but you convinced me how important it was to you with a very persuasive essay, complete with a design plan and everything."

"An essay?" I say with a smile. "That worked again?" I'd done the same thing when I was ten years old and wanted a hamster.

My mom smiles and shakes her head. "When your mom's an English teacher . . ." She looks around the room once more, then her eyes land on me. "I was actually really happy to have a project to work on together. It took us practically the whole summer, but it was fun to see you put your own style and personality into it." She pauses. Smiles, like she's remembering it. "You picked everything out, from the paint, to the bedding, to those cute little lights."

I follow her eyes up to the string of lights that look like little glass floats bordering the ceiling, then around the room full of shades of blues and turquoise, with little pops of red here and there. "I like it," I say, trying to imagine choosing each of these things. "It's pretty." And it really is, but there's a little pang in my chest. I want to see something that's familiar. Some remnant of my old room, with its bright yellow walls and butterfly decals over the bed. I can remember deciding in seventh or eighth grade that they were childish and I hated them, and begging my mom to let me redo my room. But I can't remember taking them down, or choosing new paint colors, or picking out a new comforter or bedside lamp. I must have, though. It's all here, and my mom says I did, and *she* remembers it.

I can feel her watching me, and I wonder if it makes her

sad to have these memories of us together that I don't. It makes me sad that it feels like it never happened. That when I try to remember it, I come up empty. Numb, almost.

"Thank you," I say, "for working on it with me."

She looks surprised. "You're welcome." She laughs and kisses me on the forehead. Pulls me in for the fifth hug since we've walked through the front door. "I'm so happy you're home."

I let my head rest on her shoulder a moment. "Me too," I say. Though it's not exactly right. It's good to be home, but the word *happy* feels like a stretch. I wanted to leave the hospital, and I wanted to come home, but I didn't realize what it would actually feel like when I got here. I didn't realize how strange it would be to see the sameness and the difference of everything, all mixed up together. It's unsettling.

My mom pulls me back by my shoulders and smiles. "Do you need anything? How's the pain?"

"I'm okay," I say.

"All right, then. I'm gonna let you get settled while I go start dinner, okay?"

"Okay."

"I was planning on tacos, but—is that gonna be too hard to swallow?"

I smile. "I'll make it work for tacos," I say. "Or guacamole, at the very least."

This makes her smile. "That's my girl," she says, closing the door softly.

I hear her walk down the hall and then the stairs. And then I'm alone. I take a deep breath, try to ignore the tightness in my ribs, then let it out in a long, slow exhale.

This is my bedroom.

The closet door is half open, so I walk over to the rack of clothes and run my fingers over the shirts and sweaters I don't recognize. Dresses I haven't picked out. A boys' water polo team sweatshirt. At first I think it's probably Sam's. I always used to steal his sweatshirts because they were bigger and cozier than mine. But looking at it, it occurs to me that maybe it's Matt's. Maybe he's a water polo player too. Maybe I stole it from him, or maybe he gave it to me. I move on without the answer.

Next to the closet is a low, wide dresser covered with brightly colored boxes and jars, some spilling out bracelets and necklaces and earrings, others that hold candles or various trinkets. I pick up a necklace and dangle it in front of me for a moment, watching the sea glass pendant spin and twist in the sunset light. It's pretty, and I wonder where I got it—if it was a gift, or if I picked it out myself. If it's something special that should mean something to me.

I make sure to put it back in the exact place it came from, like I would if I was in someone else's room, looking through someone else's things. I don't want to disturb anything, because each of these objects feels like a tiny breadcrumb, hopefully making a trail that can lead me back to myself. I want to preserve everything the way it is because Dr. Tate said that being around my things could help me remember. There's no telling which of these could be the one that does that.

I continue the tour of my room, trying to take in every little detail, hoping for something familiar—or for something to come back to me. On the opposite wall I recognize the shape of my desk, which I remember as white. Now it's painted a deep red, but the fact that it's still here, and that I know this desk, feels like a victory. Still, I approach it carefully because this new version of it doesn't quite feel like mine.

I'm curious though. I keep—used to keep—the normal desk things like pens and pencils and funny little trinkets in the top two drawers. But I saved the bottom one for special things I wanted to keep safe, and some that I wanted to keep secret: cards or notes, journals, pictures I'd taken. I had a whole photo box where I kept the shots that didn't make it onto my bulletin board—which is no longer there.

Instead, the wall above my desk is a huge chalkboard, bordered in a bright turquoise frame, every inch of it covered in different handwriting and doodles. I take a step closer and trail my fingers over it, softly, so I don't smudge any of the writing, and I realize it's not a chalkboard; it's the actual wall, painted that way. I wonder if this was my idea too.

I start to read what's written there. At first I think it must be quotes, but it's more like random thoughts, or notes, or maybe inside jokes. *The usual suspects, like scattered stars, I don't know if you got a fella but . . . , popcorn clouds, Laguna Matt!!!, customer #87, Queen Cassiopeia, your FACE!*

I read them all, over and over again, hoping that something will spark a memory, but nothing comes. Paige and Jules would know what they mean—these are probably all about them. Us. I think about calling and asking them to come over and explain them all to me, but even as I have the thought I remember that this new version of me somehow isn't friends with Jules anymore. It hits me in the chest, harder than the pain of breathing, and I wonder what happened to us. How can someone be so important in your life, and then be gone from it?

It's the same as—or maybe it's the opposite of—what happened with Matt when he came to the hospital. If what Paige told me is true about me and him—that we've been together for two years, that we're a perfect match, and that we're crazy in love, how is it possible that there wasn't a spark of anything when I looked at him?

I walk over to my bed, where there's a framed picture on the nightstand. It's of the two of us together, but it's hard to see the girl in the picture as me. She's so much more grown-up looking than I remember being. Matt's got this girl in his arms, nearly dipping her. Her eyes are closed, but she's smiling and so is he, even as he kisses her cheek. They look so happy together, I want to believe Paige. They *look* like they're in love. But I have no idea what that feels like. What I feel when I look at them—at us—is nothing.

I sit down on the edge of the bed and put the picture back in its place on the nightstand. The drawer is open just a crack, so I pull the handle and open it the rest of the way slowly, still feeling like I'm snooping in someone else's things. There are a few books and magazines stacked neatly in the corner, three tubes of lip balm, and a sleep mask that looks like a pair of sunglasses. I pick up one of the lip balms, take the lid off and sniff the fruity scent, then put it back with the others. Next, I pick up the eye mask, which is so cheesy it had to have come from one of the marina shops.

I'm about to try it on when I catch a glimpse of what was tucked beneath it. It's a small, round, nondescript case, but I recognize what it is immediately, and my heart starts to race. This can't actually be mine. I pick it up and open it slowly, hoping I'm wrong. But inside there is a circle of tiny pills around a dial at the center. I stare at the empty plastic bubbles, realizing what this means, and I almost can't breathe.

"Yep," a voice says from across the room. "You two are just a couple of little lovebirds."

I jump. Fumble with the pill pack in my hands, shove it down in the drawer and shut it before I look up.

Sam is leaning in the doorway, smirking. "I had the unfortunate experience of walking in on that once," he says with an exaggerated shudder. "Almost makes me wish I had amnesia myself."

I open my mouth to say something, but I don't know where to start. I'm immediately distracted from my brother's words by the way he looks. Logically, I'd known he was going to look different when I saw him. More grown-up, just like Paige. I thought I'd be prepared for it with him. But he looks like a different person altogether. The Sam in my mind is sixteen and gangly, and not much taller than me. This Sam, back from his first year of college, has to be over six feet tall, with broad shoulders, a scruffy face, and wild hair to match. I'm staring, I know I'm staring, but I can't get over it.

He grins and puts a hand on his chest. "My name is Sam, I live here too. I'm a genius and also your hero, so you basically worship me. And you do all my chores. And you bake me chocolate chip cookies anytime I ask. Also, Mom wanted me to bring this up to you."

He sets my camera bag on my desk and smiles, and I recognize the particular way his eyes crinkle at the corners. All at once, he's my brother again.

I get up and cross the room, and wrap my arms around

the big goof in a hug that seems to surprise him.

"Wow," he says. "You're nice now, too? This just keeps getting better."

I lean back and smack him on his chest. "Stop it."

"Well, you should be. Extra nice. Because you scared the crap out of everyone. You know that, right?" His expression is serious.

"Yeah. I got that much."

"Okay." He puts his big arms around my shoulders and gives me a gentle hug, then lets me go. "I'm glad you're okay."

"Except for that whole thing where I don't remember the last few years," I say.

He waves a dismissive hand. "It'll come back. You're probably just in shock."

"What if it doesn't?"

"Hmm," he says, stroking his chin. "There could be benefits to that. I mean, you'd get a clean slate for the most embarrassing, awkward years of your life."

"I don't know if that's a good thing."

He lights up. "No, it's actually awesome. Like some weird, do-over superpower. Do you know how many people would kill for that superpower? Think of how many things you could do over—watch *Star Wars* for the first time, read *Harry Potter*, have your first burrito from Del Sol." He raises one eyebrow. "They just opened a few months ago, and you were the one who told me how awesome they are, and now it'll be like you've never *been!*"

I laugh. "That's great, but I read *Harry Potter* in fourth grade. And we watched all the Star Wars movies on Christmas break when I was in sixth grade, remember?"

"Crap, that's right. Well, I'll keep thinking, and I'll come up with a list of awesome do-overs. We'll start with Del Sol. But maybe tomorrow, because Mom has a whole thing going on down there."

"Tacos," I say with a smile. "She told me."

"Yeah, it's a little more than tacos. She's in her usual cooking mode, so it's more like a welcome-back banquet for us and a houseful of guests."

"There's no one else coming over, is there?" The possibility makes me instantly nervous.

Sam shakes his head. "No. Paige and Matt have both been calling, but she told them it'd be best to give you a day to settle in."

"Good," I say, relieved.

We're quiet a moment, and Sam catches my eye. "It must be weird with Matt, huh?"

I nod.

"Well. For what it's worth, he's a good guy, and he really cares about you. And you care about him. And you guys are good together. So I hope it comes back, or works out, or whatever." He pauses. "I bet it will."

"I hope so," I say. But I'm not entirely sure I mean it. "And thank you."

"For what?" Sam asks.

"For being the only one to act normal around me. Can you just keep doing that?"

Sam gives a quick nod. "Absolutely. No special treatment just because you almost died and came back with do-over superpowers."

"Perfect."

He turns to go, then pokes his head back in the door. "And after dinner, if you're feeling up to it, I could use a dozen of those chocolate chip cookies you like to bake me."

"Get out," I say, and I close the door behind him.

He yells from the hallway, *"There's* the Liv I know!"

SEVEN

"SURPRISE!" MY MOM yells as I walk in.

A glittery Welcome Home banner hangs on the wall above the buffet in the dining room, huge bunches of Mylar balloons floating at each end. Below that, on the buffet, are all the flowers and cards from the hospital, and on the table in front of it all is a Mexican feast that looks like it could feed an army. Sam wasn't kidding. At least that's still the same. Mom's always cooked like we might have unexpected guests for dinner. I guess because most of the time, we do—Sam's friends, or Paige and Jules. Or we did. I don't know what we do now.

My dad comes in and puts a hand on my shoulder, then pulls out my chair. "Hope you're hungry. Your mom's just a little excited to have you home."

I survey the table. "I can tell." All my favorites are there—the makings for tacos, beans and rice, homemade salsa and guacamole, grilled corn on the cob, sliced watermelon. For the first time in I don't know how long, I actually am hungry.

We sit and start passing dishes, filling our plates. I reach for the bowl of shredded pork, and my mom puts her hand on mine. "Oh no, hon. This one's yours." She hands me another bowl with some sort of crumbled-up stuff in it.

"What's this?" I wrinkle my nose, wondering if it's a hospital-mandated thing. They did say I should stick with softer foods if my throat was still sore.

My mom looks caught off guard. "It's veggie crumbles. I made sure to get the ones you like."

Sam scoops the carnitas onto the four tortillas on his plate. "Sorry to break it to ya, sister, but you don't eat meat anymore—not even bacon."

I just look at him. "Stop it."

"I'm serious. I wouldn't joke about bacon. Ever."

I roll my eyes. "Right. I know I said be normal, but you can stop messing with me now." I almost want him to be messing with me, because I hope I would know something like that about myself.

"No, he's right, honey," my mom interjects.

Or maybe I wouldn't. "What? Since when?"

"This whole last year. Started last summer, after you watched that documentary . . . what was it called?" She looks to my dad, who just shrugs as he spoons beans and rice onto his plate. "Anyway," she says, "it's actually been good for your dad and me too. I've been branching out with my cooking, we've been eating healthier . . ."

"Thank you for waiting until I left to pull that, by the way," Sam says.

I sit there, still holding the bowl of veggie crumbles that my mom has made just for me. I don't even know what I eat anymore.

"Eat whatever you want," my dad says.

We all go quiet. I look down at the bowl of tofu, or whatever it is I'm holding. This is what the me they're talking about would eat.

"I . . ." I can feel them watching me, waiting to see what I'll do, and I decide to be that Liv.

I scoop up a heaping spoonful of the veggie crumbles and put it on my tortilla, and it's like a reassurance that all is right in their world, and dinner can go on.

We pass around the plates, spoons clinking against them as we serve ourselves, and it all seems very normal, but none of this feels normal to me. I watch everyone carefully, trying to make sure I don't do anything I usually wouldn't do, or eat anything I no longer eat. I'm relieved when no one corrects the generous scoop of guacamole I put over the veggie crumbles to make them edible.

"So," my mom says with a bright smile. "I've been doing a lot of research online about posttraumatic retrograde amnesia, and the general consensus is like what Dr. Tate said. The more you're surrounded by the familiar—people, places, and your regular routines—the better chance you have of your memories starting to come back to you."

There's a loud buzz from the kitchen island, and we all look that way as it buzzes again.

"Do you need to get that?" my mom asks my dad.

He shakes his head. "No. Not right now. This has been going on all day long."

I stay quiet, feeling like I'm missing something. The phone stops buzzing.

My mom puts her hand on mine and looks at me with her smile still in place. "Anyway, I was thinking that after dinner maybe we could get out your yearbooks? Or videos? We have all your volleyball games, and graduation, of course. And I think we may even have the video from before your last prom, when the limo picked you up and you all took pictures here."

Sam glances at me, then puts his big hand on top of both mine and my mom's, mimicking her in his good-natured way. "Or . . . we could just let her chill and enjoy her first night home," he says. "You know. Let her ease back into things."

Yes. Yes, please. I'm more thankful for my brother in this moment than maybe I've ever been.

"I mean, at least until I put her back to work."

I look at him. "What?"

"Oh, that's another thing you may not remember. As of this summer, I'm your boss."

"What are you talking about?"

Sam looks at me like I'm crazy. "Man, this is gonna take some getting used to." He smiles. "At the Fuel Dock. Where we've worked every summer for the last three years. I start back early tomorrow, since I'm home anyway."

I look at my dad. "Is he telling the truth?"

"Yes."

"We *work* together?"

"Yes."

I look at Sam. "What do I do there?"

"Mainly take orders and deliver food to the boats. But we may have to rethink that one if you don't remember your way around. We can see how it goes when you come back next week."

"Let's not get ahead of ourselves," my mom says. "She needs a few days to rest and be home, and to get reac-quainted with things." She looks at me now. "So when you're feeling up to it, maybe we can start to walk you through a few pictures of those big moments, with your friends, and with Matt . . ."

The corners of her mouth turn down, and she leaves his name hanging in the air between us all. I tense.

"I'm sorry," she says. "It's just—he's been calling, checking up on you, and asking if . . ."

If I remember him yet.

I remember his face there in the hospital, apologizing over and over, pleading with me to forgive him for not being able to get me out of the car, and not understanding why I didn't know him. I still don't understand all the details of what happened. I set my empty fork down. "Who pulled me out of the car?"

"What?" my mom asks, but I know she heard me.

"At the hospital—when Matt came to see me, he kept saying sorry that he couldn't get me out."

"I know," my mom says. "I wish he wouldn't feel so guilty about that. He's been apologizing to us, too."

I look to my dad. "So . . . who pulled me out of the car? Was it the Harbor Patrol?"

He glances at my mom, finishes chewing, slowly, then shakes his head. "No."

"Then who?"

My mom shifts in her seat. My dad clears his throat. Sam

stuffs half a taco into his mouth.

"You guys. What?" I look around the table, trying to figure out what is going on. "Who got me out of the car?"

When my eyes land on my dad, he finally answers. "A kid named Walker James. I don't know if you'd remember him."

Walker . . .

The note. I know the name from the reporter's note. But when my dad says his last name, I know it from somewhere else too. I reach back, beyond the big stretch of emptiness, to the names and faces I do remember.

Walker James . . .

"He lives on one of Charlie's old boats at the marina. Saw your car go off the bridge and hopped on a fishing boat to go help."

I try to take in what my dad is saying, but at the same time, from the place in my brain that still remembers, I can see a face. It's the face of a boy, twelve or thirteen years old—one I didn't know, but would see around school or town, always with an older group who usually hung around the skate park or outside 7-Eleven.

"Did he . . . was he the one who . . . ?"

My mind tries to form a picture from these new details, and my hand goes to my chest, where I can feel the squeeze of pain with every inhale. I remember what Dr. Tate told me about the CPR and my broken ribs. For the first time, it feels like it's something that actually happened.

My dad nods. "Yeah. He jumped in and got you out. Started CPR and kept you going until the paramedics arrived. We're lucky he was there and that he knew what to do."

"Have you talked to him? Did he come to the hospital?"

"No," my mom answers. "He didn't come to the hospital. But your dad and I went to see him a few days after the accident, and we let him know how grateful we are for what he did." She smiles at me. "Can you please pass the hot sauce?"

It's right next to my hand, but I don't reach for it. "Wait, that's it? What if I want to say thank you? I *should* say thank you."

My mom gives my dad a look that very clearly says, *Help.*

He gets the message, along with the rest of us, and leans forward on both of his elbows. "Tell you what. Let's focus on getting you well and strong again, and moving forward. This town is small enough that I'm sure you'll see him around, and you can thank him when you do."

"It *was* pretty badass, what he did," Sam says, taking down the other half of his taco in one bite. "It didn't even look like he—"

"*SAM.*" The urgency in my mom's voice snaps all our

eyes her way. "Can you please pass the tortillas?" she asks, even though there are plenty on her plate.

"Oh. Sure." He holds the tortilla warmer out to my mom, and I see her give him a look now. Only, this one I can't read. He shrugs an apology.

I try to figure out what just happened, what I'm missing, because it feels like we're back to that game of catch-up that I'm beginning to hate. Then I remember what the hospital volunteer had said, and I know there's something my mom is trying to keep from me.

"Is there a *video* of the accident?" I ask.

They all go still.

"Did someone film it?"

My parents look at each other, have a conversation with just their eyes. Then my dad sets his fork down and looks at me.

"There is a video, but not of the accident. A bystander caught the rescue on his camera."

"Rescue?" I let this sink in, that there is footage out there somewhere of what happened to me. "Is that . . ." I pause, trying to figure out what to ask next. "Is that why the newspeople have been around? Was it—was I on the *news*? People have *seen* it?"

My dad nods. Sam stays quiet. My mom reaches out her hand to mine and I take it away.

"Why didn't you tell me this?" I ask. My voice is shaky with anger.

"We didn't want to overwhelm you, sweetheart." She looks to my dad for help, then back at me. "You have so much else you're dealing with right now, and I didn't think it would be . . ." She drops her head. "I'm sorry. I thought it might be too much for you right now."

"Well, it is. All of this." I gesture to the Welcome Home banner and all the flowers, and then at the plate in front of me. "I'm not hungry anymore."

I push my chair back from the table and stand up too fast. They all look up at me, and I try not to let the pain in my chest show on my face.

"I'm going up to my room."

They all look a little unsure of what to say. Finally, my dad nods. "Okay. You need help up the stairs?"

I shake my head.

My mom reaches a hand out and brushes my arm. "If you need anything, we're right here."

"I know," I say. "Thanks."

I turn and walk out of the dining room, around the corner to the hallway where the stairs are, but I don't go up them. Not just yet. I stand in the same spot I used to stand to try to overhear whatever grown-up conversation was happening at the dining room table. And just like I remember, they have no idea I'm right there.

My mom's voice is too hushed to hear the words she speaks, but her tone is upset.

"I'm sorry," Sam says. "I didn't know she didn't know. But you're not gonna be able to keep her in a little bubble forever. The accident made national news. The first time she goes anywhere or talks to anyone or turns on her computer, she's gonna find out about it."

"Oh my God, I should've taken her computer out of her room."

I hear my mom's chair slide across the hardwood floor and I practically leap up the first step, but my dad's voice stops me.

"Suze, stop. He's right. We can't protect her from everything. She's gonna see the video at some point. And it'll be okay." He sighs. "Let's take it one day at a time. Liv's home, and she's safe, and that's what's most important right now. I've got a guy on every shift looking out and making sure nobody bothers us here at the house. Shouldn't take more than a day for things to calm down, and for the media vultures to lose interest. We'll figure out the rest as we go, okay?"

My mom's answer gets lost in the sound of a chair moving against the floor again, and plates clinking together, and I know I have to go. Now. I climb the stairs as quick as I can, and I feel every step in my ribs, but I don't stop until

I get to my room and close the door behind me.

It takes me a moment to catch my breath, and for the pain to subside. Once it does, I cross the room as quietly as I can, sit down at my desk without making a sound, and switch on my computer.

EIGHT

I START TO type my name into the search bar. "Olivia Jor . . . ," and the auto search fills in the rest:

Olivia Jordan drowning

Olivia Jordan car accident

Olivia Jordan hospitalized

Olivia Jordan dead

A chill runs through me.

There are what look like headlines: "Accident on Carson Bridge, Teens Rescued from Submerged Car," "Teen Pulled From Harbor in Miraculous Rescue . . ."

The list goes on, but my eye goes immediately to the link with a dark, indistinguishable thumbnail image next to it, and a video time of three minutes, fourteen seconds in the bottom corner. I have a strong, certain feeling that this is the video my mom doesn't want me to see, which makes me feel even more certain that I *need* to see it.

Still. I hover over the play arrow with the mouse for a long moment before I click, afraid to know why. I wait. Breathe. Tell myself that it'll help to see it.

And then I click.

The video takes a moment to load, and I hold my breath as I watch the circle spin.

And then it starts abruptly, and too loud.

There's yelling. The echoing rush of wind. And feet, running on the wooden planks of the bridge. The camera jumps around, shaking wildly, and it makes me a little dizzy.

"Oh my God," a voice says off camera. I don't recognize the voice, but I can hear the panic in it. "Call 911!"

The running stops, and the camera swings up from the ground. The railing of the bridge goes by in a quick flash, and the guy holding the camera finds the water. The camera shakes as he catches his breath, finds what he's looking for, and focuses.

It doesn't look real.

The night and the edges of the screen are inky black, but the water of the harbor is lit with the lights from the bridge. And from beneath? At first I can't figure it out, but then the words from the story I've been told, and from the search screen, come back to me and I understand. The greenish circle of light shining beneath the surface is from the headlights of the submerged car. My car.

There is more yelling. Splashing in the water. An empty boat drifting just off to the side of where the car is sinking.

The camera zooms in on the splashing, and I can make out a person swimming—no, two people. They make it to the boat, and one pushes the other one up the side, dumping him onto the deck. Now the camera gets even closer, and I can see that the person lying on the deck of the boat is Matt. He lies still on his back for a moment, but then sits up and coughs and retches seawater. Still coughing, he grabs the side of the boat and pulls himself to his feet, then leans over and points frantically, trying to yell to the person who's still in the water.

The wind drowns out his words, but the camera swings back to where he's pointing, back to the sinking car, where the other person is already swimming.

"Holy shit," the voice behind the camera says. "I think there's someone else in the car. There's someone still down there."

I watch as the swimmer dives back down under the water. For a moment, I can see a blurry silhouette in the eerie green light, but then it disappears completely. Seconds tick by, and I wait, along with the person filming, for him to come back up. It seems like he's under the water for an impossibly long time, when all of a sudden he breaks the surface.

I strain to see if he's come up with the other person, but it's just him.

He takes a big breath and dives back under. Time slows down. One . . . two . . . who knows how many seconds go by. I'm holding my breath, suffocating right here in my bedroom, waiting for him to come back up, and it makes me wonder if I tried to hold my breath at all, or if I even knew what happened. If I was even conscious when we hit the water.

After what seems like forever, two heads break the surface. One of them scrapes his way to the boat, dragging his heavy load to where Matt stands helpless, hands on top of his head, raking through his wet hair over and over.

I inhale sharply. Wince both at the pain, and the image on the screen.

The girl Walker James pulls from the water is dead. That's what anyone would say, looking at her.

The camera zooms in, shaking a little, and she comes into focus. Even in the golden lights shining down from the bridge, her skin is an unnatural shade of blue. Her top hangs loose and heavy with water from one shoulder, revealing a black bra strap. Long, dark hair streaks down her face in waves, covering her eyes, nose, mouth, and I want one of them to brush it away so she can breathe easier, but the blue of her skin says it doesn't matter. She isn't breathing. She can't feel the hair covering her face, or the water that moves in her lungs instead of air.

She can't feel anything.

Not his arms that drag her dead weight from the dark water, or the crack of her skull against the boat as they lift her into it. Not his hands that lay her down roughly on the deck, then search her neck, her wrists, anywhere, for a pulse. She doesn't feel the bite of the night air against her bare skin when they rip her shirt open, straight down the center, without hesitating.

I watch, relieved that she can't feel the force of those hands as they come together, one on top of the other, in the middle of her chest, and thrust downward. Deep enough to produce a contraction in her motionless heart. Hard enough to send a rush of blood and oxygen through her body, to her brain. Strong enough to crack her ribs.

I wince at this, and at those hands, that come down again and again, the full weight of the person behind them compressing her chest, her lifeless body convulsing under the force of them each time. Over and over.

I think I might be sick.

But then, like a reprieve, the hands stop, brush the hair from her face, almost gently, and tilt her chin to the sky. The camera zooms in on her face just as he pinches her nose and brings his mouth to her blue lips. He breathes his own air into her lungs before his hands move back to the center of her chest to start the cycle again.

This time they come down harder. His movements are less controlled. The compressions more powerful.

Matt paces frantically, hands still running through his hair.

Then something stops him still.

He yells something at Walker, then takes a few steps toward him.

Walker doesn't even look up. Just keeps at the compressions. Doesn't see Matt coming.

Matt yells something again, then goes at Walker with the full force of his body. The impact knocks them both to the deck of the boat, and they tumble, away from my body. Walker comes out on top, cocks a fist back, and swings hard and fast. One punch, and then he's back to his feet, and then down on his knees, next to where I lie, motionless.

And then, in stark contrast to what he just did to Matt, he brings his mouth back to mine and breathes air into my lungs before he starts again with the compressions.

Matt lies in a crumpled pile a few feet away.

Sirens whine in the distance. Voices off camera murmur urgent words that are lost in the wind. Someone is crying.

"My God," the voice from behind the camera says. "There's no way she's going to live."

Another off-camera voice weighs in. "She was down

there way too long. That girl's too far gone."

It cuts off, just as abruptly as it started.

I sit there, staring at the blurry black screen and catching my breath.

And then I get up, check that my door is closed all the way, turn my light out, the volume down, and restart the video. I watch it all again.

And again.

I watch it over and over, each time trying to feel something, anything. I watch it until I have it memorized, second by second, frame by frame. Walker getting Matt onto his boat. Walker diving down and coming back up with my limp body in his arms. Walker bringing his lips to mine, trying to breathe life back into me.

This. This makes me feel something.

It's intimate. And he's just as much a stranger to me as Matt is, but after seeing these things, I don't want him to be. I want to know him. Or thank him, at the very least, regardless of what my parents say. I owe him that much.

I search his name next.

I double-check my search, because the list of results that comes up is almost identical to the one displayed when I searched my own name. It's as if the accident was the point of intersection where our lives converged, when they otherwise wouldn't have.

I read every article, watch every news clip I can find, and

each one offers almost the same details—that he was bringing a boat into the harbor, saw the accident, and jumped in to help. They all use the same pictures, mostly blurry screen captures from the video clip. One article has a different shot, though. It's of a gurney being loaded onto an ambulance, presumably with me on it, but it's hard to tell. There's a small crowd of people in the background, and I zoom in, searching for a glimpse of Walker. I find Matt, sitting on the ground with one of those shiny silver blankets around his shoulders as a paramedic examines something on his arm. I scan the rest of the photo for Walker but don't see him anywhere at first. I'm about to give up when I spot him at the very edge of the shot. He stands alone, off to the side, arms crossed over his chest, wet clothes clinging to him. Watching the gurney as it's being loaded into the ambulance.

And that's it.

There are a few follow-up stories that mention an investigation into what caused the accident, but that's all. There's nothing else about Walker anywhere. No interviews, not one quote from him. No social media pages, or tagged photos. Nothing.

Like until the night of the accident, he didn't exist.

NINE

THE NEXT MORNING, I find my mom bent over the dining room table, in the same clothes she was wearing yesterday.

"Did you stay up all night?"

She jumps, then turns around, hand on her chest, and I can tell by the bags under her eyes that the answer is probably yes.

"You scared me," she says. "I didn't even hear you come down the stairs."

"I'm stealthy," I say, walking stiffly over to the table. "What are you doing?"

She turns back to the table and puts her hands on her hips. "I pulled everything out last night and started putting it in chronological order, but then I ended up looking through it all. Kind of taking my own trip down memory lane, I guess." She smiles, but she looks exhausted. "Maybe it's time for a break. And some coffee."

"Do I drink coffee now?"

"No," she says. "Not anything I count as coffee, anyway." She puts a hand on my shoulder. "Come on. Let's get you something to eat before you take your antibiotics."

We walk into the kitchen and she goes to the refrigerator. "Did you sleep okay? Better than in the hospital?" She pours a glass of juice and slides it across the kitchen island to me, and I sit down on one of the stools.

I take a sip, and the images that played over and over in my mind all night—of the black water, and Matt, and Walker, and my body on the deck of his boat—flash through my mind. "I slept great," I say, as brightly as I can. I don't bring up the video, and neither does she.

She reaches over and tucks a strand of my hair behind my ear. "Anything come back? Now that you're home?"

I look down at the counter. "Nothing that I don't already remember from before," I answer, feeling the failure in my response.

"That's okay," she says gently. "It's probably just going to take some time."

Neither of us raises the other possibility, that maybe it won't come back at all, but I'm certain we can both feel it, hovering in the air above us.

My mom doesn't let it hover long. "So Sam and Dad are at work already. I've done everything humanly possible to get someone to cover my workshop today, but no one is available, so I have to go in—just for a few hours." She looks at me, apology written all over her face. "Will you be okay here alone? Maybe I should just cancel it."

"Don't do that," I say. "I'll be fine."

"Are you really sure? I hate to leave you at all on your first day home. Maybe you should invite Paige to come over. So you're not alone."

"It's my second day home. Don't worry. I'll be fine. I don't need a babysitter." She looks at me carefully, and I can tell she's still on the fence. "Didn't Dr. Tate say something about getting back to our lives? I think that was supposed to include you too."

I say this to make her feel better about leaving—because a big part of me wants her to go so I can be alone here, in our house. So that I can examine it like I did my room, without anyone watching.

She takes a deep breath and lets it out. "You're right." She looks at her watch. "Shoot. I don't even have time to shower. You *sure* you'll be okay? Really. I can just cancel. People would understand."

"Mom. I'll be fine. Go. I'm still pretty tired, so I'll probably just rest most of that time anyway."

She nods and glances at the dining room table, where the yearbooks and photos are all laid out neatly. She's even labeled them with a different-colored Post-it for each year.

"And if I get bored, I have those to look through," I add.

She seems reassured, even encouraged, by this, so I don't tell her that going through years of memories I don't have is something I'd really rather do on my own. For the first time, anyway. Like watching the video.

"Okay," she says, nodding like she's trying to give herself the final push to believe her answer. "But if you need anything, or if something happens, you call me—oh! That reminds me. Your dad went out last night and got you a new phone." She smiles. "You have the nicest one of all of us now," she says, crossing the kitchen to the counter next to the fridge. She unplugs a sleek silver iPhone and grabs the shopping bag next to it, then brings them to me.

"Here you go. He set it up already. It's got our numbers and Sam's, Paige's, and . . . and Matt's—just in case." She pauses. "It's a new number, so nobody but Dad and Sam and I have it yet. That way you won't . . . get any unwanted calls."

The way she says it makes me think that she's not just talking about Matt. I think of the way Dad's phone rang off the hook during dinner last night, and then of the card from Dana Whitmore, with her number on it, stashed in my dresser drawer.

"Thank you," I say, taking the phone from her.

She eyes me carefully. "Do you . . . remember how to use it?"

I look down at it in my hand. As far as I remember, this is the first one I've ever had. Not that I don't know how to work it. I flash on a memory of playing with the one Paige got as a gift for eighth-grade promotion. I remember the quiet envy I'd felt because my parents still were still digging in their heels about getting me one. I click the home button, and the screen appears. "Yes," I say quietly. "Thank you," I add, scrolling through my five contacts.

"You're welcome, honey." She takes one last sip of coffee. "Okay, I really should get going." She turns my stool so we're face-to-face. "One last thing—and this is important. Don't answer the house phone, and if anyone comes to the door—anyone you don't know—don't answer that either. And give your dad a call and let him know right away."

I look at her for a long moment and think of so many questions I want to ask, but I know if I ask them they'll make her nervous and she'll probably decide to stay home, and I really do want to be alone right now. I need space to think.

"Okay," I say.

"And call me. For anything. I'll be home right away."

"Okay." I stand up and put my hands on her shoulders,

steering her toward the stool at the end of the counter where her purse is hanging.

"And make sure you eat a little something with your medicine so you don't get queasy. I stocked the fridge and pantry with all your favorites—I mean the things you normally ate and liked—before. But it's okay if that's changed. If you want something different, just call or text and I'll pick it up on the way home, okay?"

"Okay." I smile. "I'll be fine, Mom. I will. Go."

Her eyes well up, and she shakes her head like that'll somehow keep the tears from coming. "All right. I'm going." She pulls me into a hug. "You are so strong, Liv, and I am just so . . ."

I hug her back. "I love you. Now go to work."

She nods into my shoulder. "Okay."

We part, and she grabs her purse and keys, and I walk her to the door. After she steps out, she waits for me to close and lock it like she used to when I was little and she started leaving Sam and me for short times to go the grocery store, or run some other errand. I make sure the lock clicks into place, just like I used to do. Satisfied with that sound of safety, she heads down the walkway to her car.

I wait for her to get inside and pull away before I turn from the window and look around the quiet living room in the empty house that is familiar but not, at the same time.

And then I decide to try to find some answers.

I walk over to the dining room table where my mom has tried to help me. Spread over the entire length of the table are my high school years. My lost years. There are four rows—each neatly labeled with Post-its detailing the year and my grade in school, along with its yearbook and corresponding family photo book.

I recognize the photo books and am happy that this hasn't changed. Since Sam was born, my mom has made one every year. The older ones, from when we were babies, are actual scrapbooks with the fun paper and little cardboard shapes and stickers and themes, but I think that got to be too much to keep up. Somewhere along the way, she switched to annual photo books, the kind you upload your pictures into and create the layouts, and then it arrives all put together, shiny and finished, and bound with the year embossed on the spine.

These books are a big deal in our house because they're a big deal to my mom. There are very few pictures of her childhood and her family, neither of which was very happy, so she's always made a point to document that ours have been. She's almost never without a camera when we're all together, and she's always snapping away—candid shots when we're not looking, trying to capture something that might otherwise go unnoticed. She's the one who taught me about photography, about the magic of capturing a moment just right. And even though she'd since bought a digital camera, she always said that there was something she liked more about actual film. Something special, which couldn't be replicated digitally.

I think that was why, when I'd asked for my analog camera for my thirteenth birthday, she'd gone outside her normally frugal self and gotten me a nice one. I'd read the instruction booklet cover to cover. Learned how to thread the film and use the different aperture settings. How to take the time to really *see* what the camera lens would see. But my favorite part was always the moment of surprise when I finally got to see what I had captured when the film was developed.

I think she felt the same way about her photo books when she was finished. I think she liked to see the span of what had developed over the course of each year.

I sit down with the first photo book on the table, which begins with the second half of my eighth-grade year. I flip through pictures I remember—New Year's with just me and Sam and Mom. Dad almost always works the New Year's Eve shift, so it was just the three of us. The opening shot is of Sam and me on the couch in shiny party hats, raising our glasses of Martinelli's sparkling cider and blowing on noisemakers in the glow of the TV. I remember him being so mad that he had to stay home that year when his friends were starting to go to parties. But there was no convincing my dad, and secretly, I was happy Sam was there. As much as he bugs me sometimes, he always makes things more fun.

Next is my birthday, in February. I remember this too. There's a shot of Paige and Jules and me, scarves looped loose and bright around our necks, holding on to each other for balance at the skating rink. We're laughing so hard there were probably tears running down our cheeks, pink with the cold. I don't remember what we were laughing about, but I do remember the *feeling* of that day, of turning fourteen and celebrating with my two best friends, and thinking we'd always be together like that. Again, a pang of sadness at the loss of Jules hits me. I need to find out what happened—to find her—because it doesn't feel right that we're not friends anymore.

I flip through the next few pages of events, and land on our spring break family camping trip up the coast in the motor home. All of us but Sam got deathly sick and spent most of the trip inside that motor home, but you wouldn't know it from the pictures. There we are, standing among the towering redwoods, and there we are sitting around the campfire. There we are, our silhouettes watching the sun set over the ocean. It must've been hard to make that trip look good in the book, but Mom did. She chose the very best moments and made them the only ones for anyone who hadn't actually been on the trip. Like a highlight reel.

I don't really think about it too much until I flip past Fourth of July, and a whole summer spent on the lake, because that was the year we got a new boat. These are pictures and experiences I remember—Sam and me screaming on the inner tube, jumping off rocks into blue-green water, wakeboarding until the wind came up and the sun set behind the golden hills. Looking at them, I can smell the sunscreen, and feel the heat, and the freedom of summer—the joy of it. These moments are there in my mind, and being able to call them up from memory is a comfort. I sit there awhile, soaking in this feeling, before I turn the page, ready for another memory to unfold.

But that's not what happens. In the series of photos on the next page, Sam and I are standing on the front porch with these silly little chalkboard signs Mom made us use for this same photo every year, since the time he started kindergarten and I started preschool. Our First Day of School photo. There we are holding our chalkboard signs, Sam's with "Eleventh Grade," and mine with "Ninth Grade," written on them.

I look at myself. Examine my summer-lightened hair and sun-freckled nose, my big smile, and what must've been a completely new and carefully chosen outfit, from my red backpack all the way down to the little brown boots on my feet.

Though this is the me I remember being, the one I expected to see when I looked in the mirror, I have no memory of this moment, or the night before it, or anything after that, until I woke up in the hospital. I don't know what I felt like, standing there on the front step on the first day of high school. I don't remember if I was more nervous or excited. I don't know how many outfits I tried on before I settled on that one, or if I talked to Paige and Jules the night before. All of that is behind-the-scenes, cutting-room-floor stuff. The stuff you know only because you remember.

This is as close to the beginning of the time I've lost as I'm going to get.

I flip the pages, through fall, and pumpkin picking, and my first Homecoming dance. Jules is still in these pictures, and I'm relieved. And then it's Thanksgiving and Christmas, and I'm smiling for the camera in all these photos, in all these moments, and I don't remember a single one. I can't feel them the way I could with the earlier photos. I go through the next year, and the next. I move on to my yearbooks and go through each of them, one by one.

I'm surprised to find I'm on a lot of the pages. Student Council and volleyball, art and photography clubs—at least freshman year. I seemed to give up art club and photography after that. I show up in some random candids. Paige and Jules are by my side in a few, and then it's just Paige. I look for Jules and find her among my class, follow her school photos along with mine and Paige's, and I can almost see when we went our separate ways.

It's funny how even in a school as small as ours, the things you're a part of seem to define and separate you. Paige and I dropped art and photography, and she stayed. We stuck with volleyball and Student Council, and she joined the yearbook staff and started a student magazine. We all went to the same school, but by the end, it looks like that's all we did together.

And then Matt comes into the picture—literally. In my sophomore yearbook, his school photo is there, and I know from Paige that it's the year we started dating, but I don't know how we met or what he said to me or how we began. He's all over the yearbook too—water polo and swimming, track and Student Council. Maybe that's how we met. I try to picture it—the me I remember, sharing a class with the cute boy in the picture. Maybe we sat next to each other and he said something sweet that made me laugh, or maybe we spotted each other across the room, and there was a spark right away. Maybe there were butterflies. I don't know. Did he take me on a first date? Ask me to one of the dances we put on? Where and when was our first kiss? Who said "I love you" first? I don't know the answers to any of these questions. But I do know that he seemed to genuinely care about me at the hospital, and that he seemed just as genuinely hurt that I didn't know him. That makes me want to know him, and who we were together. It makes me want to know more about what happened on Walker's boat.

And then there's Walker. The only picture I can find of

him is in my freshman yearbook. In it, he doesn't smile, just stares past wavy, disheveled hair at the camera like he's looking right through it. And then he's gone, just like last night. He isn't anywhere. I wonder if he moved away and came back, or maybe he dropped out. Maybe he got in trouble. I search his picture like it'll give me an answer, but there's nothing. All I know of him is that we went to school together until ninth grade, but I wasn't friends with him then. And that he pulled me out of a sunken car, breathed air into my lungs, and saved my life—which makes me want to know him now.

That, at least, I can do something about.

But as I sit here looking over years of my life that I don't remember, it starts to hit me what I've really lost. A photo takes a fraction of a second to snap. Even if I added up all the time, in all the photos, from all these years, it probably wouldn't amount to more than a few minutes of my life. What about all the unrecorded moments? All the thoughts and feelings. Times I laughed until I couldn't breathe, or cried myself to sleep. Things I dreamed of, and secrets I kept. These are the things that make up who we are, and these are the things I'm worried I won't get back.

Unless I can.

Unless I can find them the way Dr. Tate mentioned, by getting back to the familiar. The routines of my life.

I make up my mind then, that that's what I'll do. I'll step

right back into my life, like it was before. And when I don't know what that was like, I'll find out. And maybe this will work. Maybe things will come back to me and I'll feel like myself again.

This feels better, having a plan. Hopeful, even.

I get up and go to the kitchen island, where I left my new phone.

"Paige?" I say when she answers. "It's Liv. Can you come over today?"

TEN

AFTER I HANG UP with Paige, I go upstairs to get ready. I shower quickly, doing the best I can to wash my own hair. I know Paige already saw me in the hospital, but I feel a little nervous about seeing her again, and I want to look like I'm doing better than I was there. More like me.

In my room, I open and close drawers, finding my way to my clothes. None of them are familiar, so I settle on a tank top and comfy shorts that I hope I would normally wear. All this tires me out a little, and my ribs are beginning to ache, but I go back into my bathroom, find a comb, and stand in front of the mirror. It's still a little foggy from my shower, so I grab a towel and wipe the space in front of me.

This new reflection stops me every time I see it. Of

course I'm taller than I remember being, but my body is different too. Somewhere in those four years, I grew the same curves I'd look at on other girls and hope for. All these differences were startling at first, but now that I'm dressed in my own clothes instead of the hospital gown, and the bruises on my face are starting to fade a little, I can almost see that this is me. This version of myself doesn't seem so far-fetched. I might even get used to her.

I finish combing my wet hair just as the doorbell rings, and I take one last look in the mirror before I go down to answer it. This is going to work. Paige is going to tell me everything I need to know, and I'm going to listen to every word so I can pick up where I left off.

"Wow," Paige says, surveying my life laid out on the table for me. "Your mom must've stayed up all night to do this."

"I think she did."

Paige runs her eyes over the yearbooks and family photo books. "That was really sweet of her."

"I know. I think she feels kind of helpless, so she's trying to do what she can."

"Well, I think it's a good idea—and you have a good plan. She gave you the outline version, and I can fill in the rest. Because you know the *actual* details of your life and relationships are gonna be a *little* bit different from the ones your mom knows." She winks and gives me a conspiratorial smile that makes it seem like I should understand what she's referencing.

For the first time, I'm a little nervous about what I might find out. "It can't be that different," I say. "Right?"

Paige shakes her head. "No. It's not. It's just that, you know. You show a different side to your friends than you do to your parents. That's all I meant." She puts a gentle hand on my shoulder. "Don't worry. There aren't any big skeletons in your closet or anything—I mean, not unless you count the time we swiped those leftover Lime-A-Ritas from your mom's staff party and snuck out to meet the boys on the beach for an illegal bonfire that got a little out of hand."

I have no idea what Lime-A-Ritas are, and I can't picture having an illegal bonfire on the beach, but I don't say so. I raise an eyebrow at her instead.

She shrugs. "Minor skeletons," she says with a smile. "It was a good night. But I'm getting ahead of myself." She drifts into the kitchen, past the open pantry door. "Wow, she did a lot of shopping too."

"Are you hungry? Help yourself," I say, following.

We both step into the walk-in pantry, and I watch Paige scan the shelves before she finally reaches for a bag of white cheddar popcorn and two bottles of sparkling water.

"There's Coke in the fridge," I offer.

She hands me one of the bottles of sparkling water. "We

don't drink soda anymore. Gave it up when we went veg-etarian." She smiles. "Good life choices and all."

I look down at the bottle in my hand. "Oh," I say. "Right."

I let Paige pick out a few more snack items—all of which, I'm happy to say, I like, and I know that I like—before we head up to my room.

I sit in my desk chair, and Paige lies on my bed, chin propped with her elbows. "So," she says, purposefully. "Where do you wanna start?"

I want to start with why there's only Paige and no Jules here, but that feels like something I should work up to. "I, um . . ." I look around the room, *my* room, and my eyes land on the chalkboard wall above the desk. "This, maybe? What is all this?"

Paige smiles as she pushes herself up and comes over to the desk so she's standing next to me. "It's your memory board, where we—" She stops. Looks down at me. "Wow, I'm sorry. I'm still getting used to this." She runs her eyes over the board. "You really don't remember any of this, do you?"

I stand up so we're shoulder to shoulder and start to read over words and phrases that feel just as foreign to me now as they were my first day back in my room. Then one catches my eye: *Good Life Choices!!!*

I point to it. "Is this about being a vegetarian? And no soda?"

Paige smiles. "Among other things. But you don't remember that, do you?"

I shake my head, and we're both quiet as we scan the board.

"Oh," Paige says, "what about this? It's from middle school, I think?"

I look where she's pointing:

PUT. *The toilet paper. Down.*

"Um, I don't . . ." I reach back in my mind for the context.

"It was the very first time we tried to sneak out to toilet paper a house, and your dad caught us." She laughs. "That's what he said. Over his police megaphone."

The scene blossoms in my mind as soon as she says it. "Yes! I remember!" Now I laugh too. "Oh my God, yes. He let us get all the way outside with all that toilet paper, *then* lit us up in the middle of the front yard."

"How *old* were we, anyway?" Paige asks.

"Twelve," I say, happy that I know the answer. I do because that was the summer between sixth and seventh grade, which I still remember, in great detail. A few weeks later we succeeded in sneaking out and TP'ing our crushes' houses *without* getting caught.

"That's right," Paige says. "Oh man, I thought we were in so much trouble."

I shake my head at the memory. "And Jules was so embarrassed she wouldn't come over for the rest of the summer."

We're both laughing, and there it is again. I can *feel* that moment of standing there, knowing we were caught, completely terrified of what was going to happen next, just like I can feel this moment, now. The two of us having something we share. Something that bonds us.

Our laughter fades, and I wonder if it's because she feels like something is missing the same way I do.

"What happened?" I ask. "With Jules?" So much for working up to it.

Paige looks at the floor, and then at me, her face serious now. "What's the last thing you remember? With her, I mean."

"The three of us, together, talking about starting ninth grade." I close my eyes, and I can see it, the three of us sitting here in this room. "I remember planning how we were gonna decorate our lockers, trying to figure out what our chances were of having at least one class together. Hoping it would be PE so we could hide behind each other to change. Being excited and scared all at once." I open my eyes and look at Paige now. "I remember being friends. All of us."

Paige is silent.

"What happened to us?"

She looks down at her hands. Won't meet my eyes.

I wait, hoping the silence will give her the space to explain.

After a long moment, she looks at me. "Honestly? It's been so long I don't even remember." She shrugs. "It was just one of those things where she started hanging out with us less and less, and we just sort of . . ." She looks down, picks at fuzz on my comforter. "Drifted."

"But *how*? I don't understand. Why would we let that happen?"

"I don't know. It's hard to explain." She looks at me now. "There wasn't any big fight, or anything like that. It was just . . ." She takes a deep breath and lets it out in a sigh. "Sometimes people just change, Liv. It's sad, but that's what happened. There wasn't anything we could do about it."

I think of Jules, and of the three of us together, and no matter how hard I try to accept what Paige is saying, it doesn't feel right.

I'm not ready to let it go just yet, but Paige claps her hands together. "So," she says. "What else? You want me to tell you everything I know about you and Matt, and how you guys are meant-to-be cute?"

"No—I mean, I do. Just. There's something else I . . ." I glance at my computer. "I saw the video. Of me, and the rescue and everything."

Paige's eyes widen. "Oh Jesus. Why'd they show you that? How completely traumatizing."

"Nobody showed it to me. I found it myself."

"It's awful," Paige says. "I couldn't watch it."

"I watched it. Over and over."

"Why?"

I shake my head. "I don't know. So it would seem real? So I could understand why my parents acted so weird when I started asking them questions about it."

"You almost died, Liv. You don't think they're gonna be a little freaked out about the details of that?"

"No, I get that. They just acted strange when I asked about Walker being the one who pulled me out."

Paige sits back and waves a dismissive hand. "Oh. That's probably because of the whole thing that happened with your mom."

"What thing with my mom?" I ask slowly.

Paige takes a sip of her sparkling water. "When we were freshmen. He was in her class, and he was out a lot, and then when he'd come back, he'd look like he'd gotten beat up. She asked us about it, and we told her what we'd heard— that it was his dad. So the next time he missed a bunch of school and came back with a broken arm, she called and reported it, and it turned into this whole big thing."

"How? What do you mean?"

"Just . . . his mom came to the school all angry and yelled

at your mom in the parking lot, saying how she ruined her life, and calling her all kinds of names. Your dad ended up having to come down and arrest her, and they filed a restraining order against his mom and all that. You know. Super-classy, small town drama."

I realize that this was years ago for Paige, probably a blip on her radar, but she's so casual about it. I try to be too. Try not to be entirely freaked out. No wonder my parents acted the way they did when I brought up Walker.

"What happened to Walker?" I ask, anxious that there may be more.

Paige shrugs. "I don't know. He was gone after that. At first he went to live with relatives or something, but then I think he ended up in a group home until he got emancipated."

"So my family broke up his family?"

Paige shakes her head. "No."

"It seems like it," I say, remembering his yearbook picture.

"They didn't. His parents were a mess. I'm pretty sure they both ended up in jail, which is probably why your parents acted like that about him—even after what he did. He's the kind of guy it's just better to keep your distance from, you know?"

I nod. "Yeah. I get it," I say. But I don't. Not really. It

seems sad and unfair. I'm about to say this to Paige, but there's a knock on the door.

"Come in," I say, and my mom does.

"Oh, Paige—hi, honey! I'm so glad you're here." She looks at me and smiles. "I guess we survived me being away for a few hours, didn't we? Everything okay?"

"Yes we did, and yes it is."

"Good. Well, I'm back now. You girls let me know if you need anything." She looks at Paige. "Will you be staying for dinner?"

Paige looks at me.

"Yes," I say. "We still have lots of catching up to do."

This seems to make them both happy.

"You girls good with pizza? I can have Dad grab a couple on his way home from work."

"I'm GREAT with pizza," Sam's voice says from the hall. He appears in the doorway. "Just as long as it's from First Class. With light sauce. And extra cheese."

My mom rolls her eyes. Sam has always been particular about where he eats, and I guess some things never change.

"I'll put your request in with your dad," my mom says. And then she goes.

Paige laughs, and Sam comes into my room in his Fuel Dock uniform, which consists of a baseball hat and T-shirt with the logo printed on them, and a pair of shorts.

"What's up, girls? How goes the trip down memory lane?"

He plops himself onto the bed next to Paige, props his chin in his hands, and bats his eyelashes.

"You're such a dork," I say.

Paige gives him a playful shove. "Go away. You weren't invited. And you smell like grease."

"I prefer to call it eau de French fry," he says, smelling his shirt. He grins at me. "Did she tell you how you totally embarrassed yourself at prom?"

Paige shakes her head. I give him a look, almost positive he's messing with me.

Sam remains both undeterred and completely entertained by himself. "Or what about the time you accidentally mooned everyone at the rally?"

"What?"

"Stop it," Paige says to him. "Now he's just making things up."

Sam raises his eyebrows at me. "Ooh. Did she get to the part where she got buzzed and totally tried to make out with me last summer before I left for school? 'Cause that was unexpectedly awesome."

"Sam!" Paige shoves him so hard he rolls onto the floor. "Shut *up*." She looks at me, hands pleading innocence in the air. "That's not how—that did NOT happen, I promise."

Sam gets up, smile still on his face, and shrugs. "Okaaay . . . everybody's got their own version of the truth, I guess."

"And his is wrong," Paige says flatly.

Normally, I'd believe her without question, because the idea of the two of them is weird and gross, and I can't imagine a world where Paige would try to kiss my brother. But there's a half second where her eyes flick to him, and there's something there that makes me wonder.

"You guys *kissed*?"

They go silent, but their expressions say it all.

"Ugh. I don't . . . I don't even wanna know," I say.

Sam looks at Paige. "Oh, I think you do."

She looks at me apologetically. "We were both a little drunk. It was just a kiss." She glances at Sam. "Then I came to my senses."

I'm sure there's more to the story, and maybe even more between them, but I don't want to go any further down that road—at least not now—so I bring up the other thing she said that caught my attention.

"You've been *drunk*?" I say, like it's something she could get in big trouble for.

Paige and Sam look at each other now, clearly trying not to laugh.

"Have *I*? Do Mom and Dad know?"

Now they lose it. The idea of it is honestly a little scary to me, and it must show on my face, because Paige comes over to where I'm sitting and puts her arm around my shoulder. "Once or twice. And you were cute. Just got a little silly, is all. And no, I don't think Officer Jordan knows."

I try to add this to my mental picture of myself, which is becoming more and more paradoxical. I've been drunk, but I've never had a sip of alcohol. I have birth control pills in my nightstand, but I've never . . .

"Wow," Sam says, catching his breath. His phone buzzes in his pocket, and he takes it out and checks it, then looks at Paige, suddenly serious. "You fill her in on Matt yet? Poor guy keeps texting." He looks at me now. "He's worried. He wants to see you, Liv."

"We were getting to that," Paige says softly. "I've been talking to him a lot, and he's so worried that this means—that he's lost you—and I keep trying to tell him it'll be okay. And it will. Because you guys are so great together, and I think if you spent some time with him, you'd see why. Even if you don't remember him, you're still *you*. And I bet you'd fall for him all over again. Like a second chance."

"A do-over!" Sam says. "That's what I said!"

"Sort of. It could be all sweet and romantic. You could have all your firsts all over again. First date, first kiss, first—"

"AND THIS IS THE PART WHERE I EXIT THE ROOM," Sam says, standing up.

"Good," Paige says. "It's about time."

Sam gives a salute and leaves without closing the door

behind him. It used to drive me crazy when he did that, and I'd always yell at him to come back and close it until he did, but this time I don't get up and I don't say anything.

Paige gets up and closes the door softly, then turns and smiles at me. "Oh my God, Liv. We really do have *so* much to talk about."

ELEVEN

I SIT, STARING at the picture on my nightstand, not knowing what to feel besides relief at finally being alone again.
Paige has gone home, we're all in our rooms, and the house
is nighttime quiet, but my mind is not. It's spinning with
everything I've heard in the past few hours, trying to catch
up and process it all—a task that feels impossible.

After dinner, Paige had taken me through the entire history of me and Matt. She'd told me everything she could
remember, and it had made me feel sad, and guilty, and
somehow jealous that I didn't have a single one of these
memories for myself, while she had them all.

How he'd come new to our school in the middle of the
year from Laguna Beach, with messy hair, an easy smile,

and a friendly, humble air about him, which made every girl in our tiny high school automatically interested.

How I'd been interested too but hadn't wanted to join the crowd vying for his attention, and as luck would have it, I hadn't needed to. We'd had a class together. Math. He'd joked. I'd laughed. We'd both gotten in trouble. That class, and seeing him, were all I'd talked about that week—looks we'd exchanged, the way he'd hung back to leave so we'd walk out the door at the same time, the way he'd smiled as we parted ways for the next class, and what it had all meant.

Paige had built up the suspense before she'd told me how he'd walked up to me after school on the Friday of that first week and said: "I don't know if you've got a fella, but you wanna go out tonight?"

How I thought the word *fella* was the most adorable thing I'd ever heard.

How I'd said yes, and he took me out on my first real date because the kids in our town usually don't do that. We "hang out" instead. At parties, or the beach. But he'd taken me on an actual date where he picked me up, and met my parents, and brought me to Del's Pizzeria, a little Italian place near the beach, where he fidgeted and didn't eat a single bite because he was so nervous.

Paige told me how we'd taken a walk out on the pier after that, and sat on the top of a wooden table watching the stars come out over the ocean.

How he'd pointed out all the constellations he knew and told me the stories behind them. How the story of Queen Cassiopeia had been my favorite.

She told me how he'd dropped me off on my doorstep without so much as attempting a kiss, and I'd called Paige and told her every detail, sure that this meant he didn't like me, and that was the end of it, and I was so sad because after that night, I really liked him.

She told me how she'd said I was wrong because she'd seen the way he looked at me when he thought no one was watching.

She gloated when she told me how she'd been right because he'd called me the next day, and that we were together every day after that, and that first kiss came just a few weeks later at Paige's house, where a group of us were working on a project and the power went out, and we were alone in the dark for a few moments before it came back on.

How after that I'd told Paige I was already falling in love with him and how every day after that proved true, because we became that couple that just *fit*. The couple who were so in love you wanted to hate them, but they were so happy, you couldn't. The first ones on the dance floor at parties or dances. The last to leave.

Ours was a perfect love story, the way Paige told it.

She wove so much detail in, so intricately, there was no way she could be making any of it up. I had to have told her these things in giddy late-night phone calls and chats where we rehashed and analyzed every little detail. And there were pictures to prove it.

Paige had gone to my computer and pulled up all my social media pages, where there was picture after picture of Matt and me together—smiling, laughing, kissing, snowboarding, on the boat, at the beach. We scrolled back through three years' worth of my pictures and my captions, matched some of the stories up with the chalkboard wall, and all the while I'd tried to feel these memories like I could feel the ones I still have.

But I couldn't. And sitting here, in the quiet of my room, the only thing I feel is a strange numbness. Like my emotions are trapped beneath a thin layer of something I can't get through. Being told the story of something is not the same as experiencing it, no matter how touching or detailed it is. And now all I can think is that our perfect love story might already be over if I can't ever remember what happened for myself. I don't want it to be over, though, so I push the fear away. Try to repeat to myself what Paige said: that we fell in love once, and that no matter what happened the night of the accident, I'm still that girl who loved him, and he's still that boy who loves me. And that we'll find our way back to each other, because that's what happens when you have such a strong connection.

I'd been convinced enough—or maybe just hopeful

enough—to call him, with Paige sitting right there on the bed next to me. Matt had answered before the first ring was even finished, and when I stuttered my hello, and explained that I wanted to see him, all he could say at first was "Really?" like he couldn't believe it, and then "Thank you, Liv." The hitch in his voice had put a lump in my throat, and by the time we'd hung up, we'd made plans for the following afternoon. A first date with my boyfriend of two years.

The next morning, I wake up like I have each day since I've gotten home: I lie still, reminding myself that this is my room. As soon as I move, my body reminds me of what happened, though each day the pain is a little bit less. I've almost become used to the girl in the mirror, so I don't spend as much time in front of it as I used to. But now that I understand a few of the phrases on my chalkboard wall, courtesy of Paige, I spend more time in front of it, reading them over like some secret code that will unlock it all for me.

This morning, a note on the board that Paige didn't get to catches my eye. *Second Chance*, it says, and I think I know what it means.

When we were little, my dad used to walk me and Sam down to the harbor on Sundays, and we'd "pick out" our boats. My dad went for the fishing boats, planning his retirement as a fisherman out loud. Sam always chose the biggest, flashiest boats that belonged to wealthy summer tourists. But my favorite boat in the harbor was a beat-up old sailboat called *Second Chance*—mainly because it looked like it was waiting for one. The once-white paint on the hull was dingy and peeling away, covered in barnacles below the waterline, and the faded wood of the cabin was almost as bad. It was cracked and rotted in places after years of exposure to the salt, and sun, and weather, and the canvas covers on the boom had practically disintegrated. I used to imagine how it would look if someone actually did give it a second chance, and what it would be like to sail out of the harbor and into the wind and the open ocean, on some grand adventure.

Later, when I got my camera, one of my favorite places to shoot was the harbor, with all its sights and sounds, and water and sunlight. I'd take shots of the sea lions lounging on the buoys; the tall masts of the sailboats, silhouetted against the bright blue sky; the sun setting over the bay, boats on the horizon. But what I loved best was taking pictures of that boat—catching its profile against the sunset or zooming in on the barnacled bottom just below the water's surface. It was my favorite subject.

My eyes drift down to my desk, where my camera case sits next to my computer. I run my fingers over the case, then sit down and unsnap it. I take out the 35mm Nikon and reach for the strap to put around my neck like my mom has always drilled into me. *This is an expensive piece of equipment. Always wear the strap.* She'd let me pick out a special one that looks more like a scarf than a strap even though it was more expensive—I think because she thought I'd be more likely to actually wear it. And she was right. I always wear it when I go out to take photos.

I slide the silk loop of the strap around the back of my neck, take the lens cap off, and bring the camera to my eye, feeling the familiar weight of it in my hands, scanning the room until I have my mirror in the frame, my own reflection obscured by the sunlight streaming through the window and the camera itself.

Click.

I love that sound. It makes me feel calm and happy. I look out the window at the already sunny day and decide I want to take a walk down to the harbor. See if my boat is still there, take some pictures. Routine.

When I go downstairs, camera around my neck, and tell my mom my plan, she looks a little surprised.

"I'll be fine," I say. "Please? I know my way, and my ribs are already feeling a lot better. See?" I demonstrate by turning my torso side to side, which hurts, but I tough it out. I need to get out of the house.

My mom laughs. "It's not that. I'm okay with you going

out for a walk. Some fresh air will be good for you." She pauses, then smiles. "I just haven't seen you with your old camera for a long time."

I glance down at it. "It's not *that* old," I say.

She gives me a funny look. "No, I guess not. I bet I've still got some film stashed somewhere if you wanted to start playing around with it again. You used to love it so much. You probably still would if you picked it up again."

"What do you mean, *used to?*" I ask. "Did I stop taking pictures or something? Is that why you brought it to the hospital for me?" None of this is making any sense.

She takes a sip of her coffee, shakes her head. "I never brought it to the hospital, honey."

"It was there," I say, though doubt starts to creep in even as I say it, because of the look on her face.

"No," she says. She shakes her head. "I don't think so. And I don't remember packing it up to bring home either. Maybe you were just thinking about it while you were there, or you were . . . confused?"

"No," I say, more forcefully. I pause, replaying the memory in my mind. It *is* a memory. "It was there, with all the flowers and everything. Someone brought it to me— maybe Dad?"

"I don't know why he would've brought it," she says, puzzled.

"Maybe he thought it'd be familiar?" I offer.

"That'd be an odd choice. You haven't used it in a long time. Years, probably."

"*What? Why?*" The thought that I stopped taking pictures bothers me almost as much as the thought of me not being friends with Jules anymore.

She looks a little taken aback, like I'm overreacting. "I think you just got busy with other things, sweetheart. Between school, and volleyball, and Matt, you haven't had a lot of extra time on your hands, that's all." She reaches out and puts a hand on my knee. "And you do take a lot of photos on your phone. It's just quicker and easier than using that."

I don't say anything.

"There's no rule that says you can't start shooting film again. It'd probably be good for you." She smiles. "You used to have a pretty good eye."

We're quiet a moment, but the words *used to* seem to linger. They feel different this time, though. Different from all the other things I've been told I used to do, because taking pictures feels like something I just *do*. In the present.

"There's actually some film in here already," I say. "So can I go for a walk and shoot the rest of it?" I have that wanting-to-be-alone feeling again. Even though it hasn't worked yet, I keep thinking that if I can just sort things out in my own mind, my memories will come back to me—or at least the pieces will feel like they make sense.

My mom smiles. "Of course. Shoot it to the end of the roll, then you can drop it off at the shop. My purse is on the counter—take some cash. It'll be fun to see what's there when you develop it."

TWELVE

AT THE END of our cul-de-sac, I kick off my flip-flops and step onto the sand, digging my toes in to let the warmth really sink in. The salt in the air is stronger down here, and I can hear the low thunder of the waves just beyond the dunes.

I feel the strain of the first few uneven steps in every muscle between my ribs, so I take the trail slowly, careful not to push too hard, but more excited to see the beach with each wave that I hear. It feels good to be out here in the sunshine and fresh air, even if it is just for a walk. It takes me only a few minutes to pick my way over the trail to where the dunes melt into the wide, flat expanse of beach and ocean and sky so perfect I lift my camera and snap a shot like a reflex.

As soon as I hear the click, though, I do think about what I'm doing. I think about what my mom said, about me not having used my camera for so long, and of it being there in the hospital in spite of that fact. I know I didn't imagine it there, but like my mom, I can't figure out how or why it would've gotten there if she or my dad didn't bring it. I've quickly become used to not knowing things for myself, and to taking everyone else's word for it, but this bothers me. It doesn't feel right, and I want to figure out why.

I look out at the expanse of blue ocean, sparkling in the sun, and lift my camera again, trying for a different angle. It makes me think of a quote my mom read somewhere and then told me when I first started taking pictures. She told me to pay attention to my attention. To try to stop and notice the things that drew my camera to my eye and made me want to capture them, because those were the things that somehow meant something to me. The idea had seemed romantic to me, so I'd taken her words to heart, and almost always found my way back down the beach, and followed it all the way to the harbor, with its water and sunlight and all the boats that knew how to navigate between the two. That's where I head now.

I'll take the last few shots on the roll and bring the film

to In Focus, and maybe that will help me figure something out. It's a thin hope, but I hold on to it as I walk, pushing my pace faster than is comfortable, to match the building urgency I feel in my chest.

By the time I reach the harbor, I'm out of breath, and in more than a little pain, but the sight of boats lined up on the docks, bobbing gently in their slips, makes me smile. This place doesn't look any different. It's exactly the same, and that small thing calms me. I take the stairs down to the main walk and head down to M Dock, where *Second Chance* is. Or was. I have no idea if it's still there, but I want it to be, so badly. Something in me needs it to be.

Anticipation flutters in my chest, and when I get to the gate for M Dock, I strain to see the far end of the dock, where I remember *Second Chance* being, but there are too many other sailboats in the way. I try the handle, but the gate's locked. The dock is quiet, empty of people, which means there's no one to let me in. I jiggle the handle again, like maybe it'll open if I want it to badly enough. The metal clanks softly as I pull, but it remains locked in place.

I look down at the keypad, wishing I knew the code. And then, before I have a chance to think about what I'm doing, I reach out and punch in a series of numbers. There's a soft click, and I pull on the handle again. It opens. I stand there a moment, shocked. I don't even know what numbers I just typed in, but they worked. The gate is open.

I check again to make sure no one is looking before I slip in. Then I close the gate softly behind me and step onto the dock. It sways a little beneath my feet, which makes me smile because I remember that feeling. It used to make me nervous as a kid to feel the dock shift like that, and to see the water through the planks of wood, but it doesn't anymore. Still, I take my time, walking slowly and scanning the weathered boats as they sway lazily, tethered in their slips.

"Hey! What are you doing here?"

My heart leaps into my throat and I jump and spin back in the direction of the voice. The movement sends a sharp pain through my ribs.

An older man, dressed in fisherman's coveralls, steps off an ancient Boston Whaler and onto the dock, eyeing me suspiciously.

"I'm sorry," I say. "I just was—I wanted to see if—"

His eyes zero in on the camera around my neck. "Walker's not around. And he doesn't want to talk to any of you, anyway. So get outta here. It's old news. Find someone else to harass."

I can't think of any time anyone has talked to me like this. It's mortifying. "Oh no, I'm not a reporter, sir. And I wasn't looking for—" I stop as his words sink in. "Walker lives around here?"

I'm not sure he believes me. He doesn't answer.

I take a step forward. "I'm sorry, I should've introduced myself. I'm Liv." I extend my hand. "The girl Walker saved from the accident a couple of weeks ago?"

The old man's eyes widen. "Oh. Bruce Jordan's girl." A smile transforms his face. "I'm sorry, darlin'. I didn't realize it was you. I just thought, with the camera, that you were another one of those reporters."

"It's okay," I say. "Completely understandable." I pause, nervous all of a sudden at the possibility of Walker being somewhere nearby. But this could be my chance to meet him and say thank you. I give the old man a smile that feels as timid as I do, but I make myself ask anyway. "I just wanted to talk to him for a minute. Can you tell me where to find him?"

He frowns. "Nope. Sorry, darlin'. He took off for a couple days. Needed to get out of here after all that, I guess. That kind of thing can get to you, you know."

I nod. He has no idea. "Do you know where he went?" I ask, feeling a little braver.

"Out to the Channel Islands, is my best guess." He motions in their direction, but the thin layer of haze out over the water keeps them hidden away, like Walker is apparently trying to be. "When he gets back, I'll tell him you came by, how 'bout that? What was your name again?"

"Liv," I say. "Thank you."

I don't make a move, and neither does he, and I'm trying

to figure out if it would be strange of me to walk the rest of the way to the end of the dock, just to see if my boat is still there.

"You have a good day, Liv," the man says. He nods at the gate, and I have my answer.

"Thank you. You too, sir."

I turn and walk back toward the gate, not feeling like I have a choice, and trying not to be too disappointed about not seeing the boat. At least I know where to find Walker now. Maybe I'll try again in a few days. Or maybe when I'm working I'll run into him.

I slip out the gate and it clanks shut behind me, but I don't leave just yet. I don't know how many shots are left on my roll of film, but I want to get to the end of it, so I position my lens through the metal bars and take a long shot of the dock, and then another of a seal lounging on a nearby buoy. I look around, feeling a little lost. At the moment I don't feel particularly inspired to take any more pictures. I just want to see what's on the roll, even if it means wasting a few frames, so I turn the camera over, flip the crank up, and slowly wind the film back until the number in the counter shows zero. Then I take it out, put it in my purse, and walk.

A family of tourists comes toward me on the sidewalk, the two kids toting bags of saltwater taffy, their parents following a few paces behind, Styrofoam cups from Splash Café in their hands. It reminds me of any time we'd have friends from out of town come in. We'd bring them down here, to the Embarcadero, the quaint little part of our coastal fishing town, and walk them around to all the shops, hitting all the important spots—chowder, coffee, and the candy store, with its slabs of fudge and taffy puller in the window.

Today, my important spot is In Focus, the camera shop.

I leave Main Street and cut down Ruby Street, where it's tucked away, off the beaten path. At least I hope it still is. The owner, Chloe, had always joked that if it wasn't for me, she wouldn't be in business. I didn't think it was true, but in this town you never know. Little mom-and-pop shops like hers come and go pretty often, so I'm relieved when I see the sign still there.

The bells jingle just like they always have when I push through the door. There are no customers, and no one's behind the counter either.

"Be right with you!" a female voice calls from the back room.

"Okay!" I say. "No hurry."

I take a moment to glance around the tiny shop. Surprisingly, it doesn't look much different than I remember it, with its small variety of cameras, lenses, and accessories displayed beneath the glass U-shaped countertop. The same framed shots of Chloe's travels from around the world hang on the walls—vibrant oceanscapes, lush rain forests, stark deserts. I remember all of them. Even the same bulletin board to buy or sell used equipment, or to advertise your services, is still on the wall next to the door.

I run my eyes over the different cards and flyers, and one in particular catches my eye. It reads:

Attention Teen Photographers!
Coast Magazine *wants you to submit your photo essay for publication in our annual Young Artists' Issue! Winners will also be featured in a mounted show at the Pelican Bay Art Festival! This year's theme is: Things Unseen*

For a moment, I try to imagine what I might shoot for the contest, but then I see the deadline has already passed. The day after my accident, in fact. As far as things that I'll always remember, that date is one of them. It marks the before and after for me, dividing my life into known and unknown. I wonder if it will always feel like that. Like everything is in relation to that date.

"Hi!" The voice startles me and I feel it in my ribs. I turn, slowly.

"Liv, oh my God, honey. Come here."

I don't have a chance to, though, because Chloe comes out from behind the counter with her arms extended and gives me a big, warm hug. Then, like she realizes it might hurt, she lets go and steps back.

"How are you doing? I've been thinking of you since I heard about the accident, sending good vibes. Are you healing?"

"I'm okay." I don't mention anything about the memory loss. I choose to focus on the physical instead. "It gets a little bit better every day," I say. I feel myself smile. A real smile. I am genuinely happy to see her.

She crosses her arms and tilts her head. "Good," she says. "I'm so glad." She smiles now, and I notice the tiny crinkles at the corners of her eyes. Those are new—at least to me. Other than that, she looks remarkably the same. I think about telling her—as a compliment—but then I'd have to explain the whole memory thing, which I just don't want to get into. I like it better this way, without her knowing.

"You look pretty today," I say instead.

"Well—" She looks pleasantly surprised. "Thank you, sweetheart. You do too. Now, what can I do for you?" she asks. "Do you have more beautiful shots for me?"

"What do you mean?" I ask. A tiny hope rises in my chest.

"Like the ones you've been bringing in for the last month. You're getting so good with mood and light. They've just been gorgeous."

I want, so badly, to ask what they were. I shouldn't have to ask about my own pictures, but now I have something to look for when I get home. This feels more right than anything else has since I've woken up. I've *been* here. I didn't stop taking pictures like my mom thinks. Or even if I did for a while, I started back up again. I don't know why she wouldn't know that, or why I would've kept it a secret.

Either way, it feels like a puzzle piece that fits. It makes me even more curious to see what's on the film. I take the canister out of my purse.

"I'm not sure if they're gorgeous. Or what's even on here, really. I just found this in my camera bag and want to see what's on it."

Chloe smiles and raises an eyebrow, and takes the film. "Ooh, a mystery roll. That's always fun."

"Can we do one hour?"

Chloe frowns. "Machine was down earlier this week, so I'm way behind. How about later this afternoon—more like three or four hours?"

"Oh. Um, okay," I say, trying to hide my disappointment. "That's fine." I almost want to ask for it back and take it across town to Rite Aid, but I have no way of getting there, and Chloe's so nice I don't have the heart to ask for it back.

She hands me an envelope to fill out. "I saw your brother yesterday, and he mentioned you'd be coming back to work soon. I'll have to put in a lunch order now that their friendliest delivery person is back."

"Definitely do," I say, though I have no idea what she's

talking about. I hand her the envelope with the film in it. "I'll see you later."

"Actually, I won't be here. But I just hired a new girl, so she will be."

"Wow," I say with a smile. "Business is booming, huh?"

Chloe lifts an eyebrow. "Not exactly. But I'm taking a trip to Iceland next month, and I need someone to run the shop."

"Ah, of course."

"I was actually going to ask you, but then the whole accident happened, and I didn't—I'm just glad you're okay, sweetie. Anyway, who knows? Maybe in the future, I'll need a *second* employee." She winks. "Bye, hon."

"Bye," I say. My hand is on the door, but I hesitate. Something in me wants to tell her what's going on with me, because all of a sudden I feel like I'm lying.

"Hey, Chloe?"

She looks up from the counter.

"Yeah?"

"I . . ." I shake my head. "It was just good to see you again, is all."

THIRTEEN

I STEP OUT the door and back into the sunlight that's so bright now it gives me a headache. When I reach into my purse for my sunglasses and realize I have none, I make my way back to Main Street to stop in one of the little tourist shops for a cheap pair and kill some time. I try on a few, and since they're two for $10, I pick a couple of pairs that I like and pay for them. When I walk out wearing one of my new pairs of sunglasses, I feel hopeful. Even a little confident.

Summertime tourist season is in full swing, and the smells of clam chowder and fried seafood drift through the air. I lean against a railing watching as people pass by, coming and going in both directions. They all seem to have something to do, somewhere to go, people to be with and laugh with. It makes me glad I'll be starting work in a few days. It's better than sitting around the house. I'm not ready to go home yet, and the Fuel Dock, where Sam's at work today, is just a few docks down, so I decide to walk over and say hi, and maybe even get a shake.

When I get there, the deck is packed full and there's a line that goes around the corner of the bright yellow building. The Fuel Dock is an obligatory tourist spot, but also a favorite of locals and fishermen, mainly because they serve up the best burgers, fries, and shakes in town. Everyone has their favorite flavor, and mine is the Double Dark Chocolate Chip because it's perfectly chocolaty and has tiny chips that fit right up through the straw.

I get in the line—it moves surprisingly fast, and within a few minutes, we've rounded the corner to the front. I see Sam behind the window, and he's hustling. Calling out order numbers, checking on food, and handing it to waitresses. It looks hectic, and I get a little nervous. I look at the line that disappears around the corner behind me. I don't know if I'm quite ready for this. When I look back at the crew behind the window, Sam sees me.

"Liv! Hey! Come here!" He grabs four grease-dotted bags and motions for me to go to the pickup window.

I meet him there, and he hands me the bags.

"Thanks, but I was gonna get a shake too."

He shakes his head. "Nice try. It's not for you. We're

slammed, and I need you to take this out to . . ." He looks down at the receipt attached to the bags. "B Dock, slip eighty-seven. The Wagners' boat."

"Um . . . okay." I don't know who the Wagners are, but I know how to find my way there.

"Thanks," he says, "Oh. And you know who the Wagners are, or you should, so act like it." With that, he disappears into the kitchen again.

"Thanks for the heads-up," I say, looking down at the bags in my hand, then out at the rows of lettered docks. I guess I start work today.

B Dock is all the way at the end of the first row, so I get going. When I reach the gate and try the handle with my free hand, it's locked just like the other one was this morning. I close my eyes and try to remember the numbers I typed in at M Dock. When I put my hand to the buttons, the code comes back to me and I punch it in, but it doesn't work. I look around, but this dock looks empty too. I don't want to fail on my first delivery. I stare at the buttons again, trying to pull the right combination out of my brain. I try one, and then another, and another. I jiggle the handle. I set the bags down and jiggle the handle again, feeling more and more panicked by the second.

"Hello!" I call. "Anyone here? It's the Fuel Dock! I have your lunch! Customer number eighty-seven?"

I wait. There's no answer. And then a water balloon

comes sailing past me and splats on the cement, splashing my legs.

A little girl, maybe ten years old, comes running down the dock in her bikini, long blond hair trailing behind her. "Jackson, *don't* throw water balloons at Liv. She was in an accident, you know. You could seriously injure her."

There's a goofy laugh, and then a splash, and a boy on a paddleboard emerges from behind a boat, grinning at me. "Sorry, Liv," he says. "I wasn't aiming for you."

"Yes you *were*," the girl says, as she gets to the gate. "Don't lie. You're so dumb."

"Your FACE is dumb," the boy shoots back. He hits the water with his paddle and sends a splash of water in his sister's direction. I have a flashback of me and Sam, and almost this exact exchange. That was his favorite joke when we were kids.

The girl ignores him and opens the gate, and gives me a hug that squeezes a little too hard. "We saw you on the news. That was so scary. You almost died." Her blue eyes are wide as they look up at me.

I'm not sure how to answer, or who these kids are. They must be regular summer vacationers. One of the families who dock their boats here for a few weeks at a time. Clearly, they know me. And we're on hugging and water-balloon-throwing terms.

"Well, I didn't," I say.

"I'm glad," the girl says, holding out two neatly folded bills.

"Me too."

I take the money and hand her the bags. "How long are you here?" It seems like an appropriate, I-know-what-I'm-talking-about question to ask.

"A whole month!" Jackson shouts from the water. "And guess what? We're gonna take sailing lessons from that guy who rescued you."

My stomach does a wild flip, and goose bumps ripple over my arms. "What?"

"Yeah. He works down at the sailboats. It's gonna be awesome! He even said he'd teach me CPR, like he did on you!"

I flash on the shaky footage from the video, of Walker's arms pumping on my chest, my body jumping and falling beneath them, and I can't believe these kids have seen it. Or that they're so casual about it.

The girl looks up at me. "Are you guys friends now? Because he saved your life?"

Her question snaps me back to the conversation.

"No," I say. "We're, um, not friends."

She frowns.

"I mean, I don't know him."

"Well, you should come sailing with us one day. Then maybe you could become friends."

She's smiling, and I can see how that would make sense in her mind as a happy ending to a scary story. I smile. "That would be fun, but I have to work, so I don't know."

"Oh," she says, wrinkling her nose. "That stinks."

"Your FACE stinks!" Jackson yells from the water. "Dylan's, not yours, Liv." He dips his paddle into the water to turn himself around, wobbles, then falls in with a splash.

The girl, Dylan, bursts out laughing, and I can't help but join her. The boy comes up laughing too, and she rolls her eyes, then levels them at me. "I wish you never taught him that joke. He's been saying it since last summer."

"Sorry about that," I say, still laughing. I look at Jackson as he climbs back onto his board. "I should've known. My brother did the same thing."

"Kiddos!" a male voice yells. "You plannin' on bringing lunch back?"

"I'm coming!" Dylan yells over her shoulder. She looks at me. "See you later, Liv."

"Bye, Liv!" Jackson waves from the water.

"Bye, guys," I say, and we all part ways.

I walk back in the direction I came from, replaying the whole conversation in my head, especially her assumption that Walker and I would now be friends because of what happened. I like the way kids sometimes see things so simply, though I'm not really sure how that would actually happen.

But still. He did save my life, and it gives me a nervous, good feeling knowing that I'll probably see him around. I stop and lean on the railing for a moment, taking in the postcard image of the bay. The sun sparkles on the glassy water, setting off the tall masts of the sailboats against a cloudless blue sky.

In the far distance, the graceful arch of the Carson Bridge frames it all. It looks pretty in the daytime. So different than in the dark. I force my eyes to stay there a moment. Try to imagine night instead of the bright sunshine all around me. I picture headlights, crisscrossing the bridge, one set after another, until something goes wrong, sending one of them off course. I see the lights arc out and away from the others, their beams cutting through the empty darkness between the bridge and the water in slow motion before disappearing beneath the surface.

And then, in my mind's eye, I see a boat. Walker's fishing boat.

I blink, and it's daylight again.

My phone is buzzing. Paige.

"Hey," she says as soon as I answer. "Where are you? I'm at your house to help you get ready."

"Get ready?" I ask.

"For your date? With Matt?"

FOURTEEN

I'M SO NERVOUS I feel sick.

I look down at my outfit, sure that it's all wrong even though Paige helped me pick it out. I fidget with the strap of the sundress, then run my fingers through the sections of hair that she'd straightened and pulled over my shoulders after she'd carefully applied my makeup. That part had taken forever, and I'd gotten stiff sitting there, but she'd been determined to do enough blending to cover what's left of my bruises. When she was finally finished, she'd stood back with a proud smile.

"Perfect."

Then she'd turned me around slowly to look in the

mirror. I almost hadn't recognized myself for the second time since I woke up.

"Is this . . . ? This is what I normally look like?" I'd asked, eyeing my reflection. "This seems like a lot."

"It's not," she'd said, hands on my shoulders. "It's just that you're not used to it. But you usually do your hair and put on makeup, especially if you're going to see Matt." She'd gestured at the makeup spread out over my desk. "This stuff is all yours, Liv. I made sure not to do anything that you wouldn't have done yourself. You look beautiful, and my work here is done. I gotta get going, okay? I have work until ten, but it's gonna be dead, so call me and let me know how it goes."

"I will."

With that, she'd packed up her stuff, given me a hug, and left me alone in my house, waiting for Matt to come pick me up.

I stand up and look in the mirror above the couch for the millionth time since I've come downstairs to wait, and I tell myself that this is me. This is what I look like now. This is what I wear when I'm going out with my boyfriend.

I look down at the phone in my hand, at Matt's phone number, just a tap away. I could call him and explain that I'm not feeling well, put this off a little longer to give myself time to memorize the history of us that Paige spent last night telling me. But she was so excited when I'd decided to call him, and today when I'd called my mom to ask her if I could go out, she sounded like she was too.

"Of course," she'd said. "We love Matt."

"I know," I'd told them.

The knock on the door sets off a wave of butterflies in my stomach. I let it settle a moment before I stand up, smooth my hair and my dress, and go to answer it. Then I stop. I stand there in the entryway for one more moment and try one last time before I see him to believe what Paige said. That I'll feel a spark of something when I see him again.

And then I open the door, and he's standing right there on the step, holding another bouquet of red flowers in his hand, looking as nervous as I am. We stand there looking at each other, not sure what to say, or do. Unsure of how to be around each other. Like the strangers we are.

There are no sparks or flashes of anything, just the warm summer air and silence between us.

"Hi," Matt says, before the quiet stretches too tight. "I . . ." He holds out the flowers to me. "I brought you these."

"Thank you," I say. "They're so pretty." I look down at them and remember the note from the hospital. His, I assume. "My favorites."

He nods. I take the flowers and he plunges his hands into

his pockets, his shoulders rising into a shrug that makes him look even more unsure than he did a moment ago. "How are you?" he asks, his eyes meeting mine. "You look . . . you look better. I mean, like you feel better. I mean—"

He shakes his head, bites his lip for a second. "Lemme just start over." He looks me in the eye. "You look really pretty."

"Thank you," I say, feeling self-conscious all over again about this version of me.

"That's my favorite dress."

"I know."

"You do?" His brows lift, the tiniest bit hopeful.

"Paige told me."

"Oh," he says. They fall.

It's quiet a moment. I try to think of something to say.

"You look nice too. Better than you did last time."

He laughs.

I cringe. "Wow, sorry. I just meant that it looks like you're healing too." I motion at his arm, which is no longer in a sling. "We're both terrible at this, aren't we?"

"Apparently," he says.

This seems to relax something in us both, at least a little bit.

"So," he says, "what do you want to do?"

His tone and the tentative look on his face make me think that he's not just talking about what we're going to do right now, today, but what we're going to do about us.

I don't know what to say, so I give what I hope is an encouraging answer any way you look at it. I step forward and reach out my hand.

He smiles in relief as he reaches his own hand out to take it.

And this is how we begin again.

It's a big step up to get into Matt's truck, so he helps me up and in, then closes the door gently before walking around to his side. When he gets in, he looks over at me. "You okay?"

I nod. "Yeah, I'm fine. Good." I smile and reach back to pull the seat belt around me, but it sticks. I try again, and it sticks again.

I'm about to try again when Matt scoots closer. "That thing's tricky, remember?" A look of horror crosses his face before he even finishes saying the word. "I'm sorry, I didn't mean to—here." He leans across me and reaches for the seat belt, and I freeze at the closeness of him.

He feels it too, I think, because he also freezes, and we're face-to-face, eye to eye, and it might be romantic if the situation were different. All it would take to close the space between us would be one little shift, a giving in to the tiny pull of the other's gravity to bring us together. For a moment, he looks like he might be the one to lean in, and I stop breathing because I don't know what I'll do if he does.

But then he blinks. Swallows hard. "It's like this," he says softly. And then ever so slowly, he pulls the seat belt out until it can reach around me and leans back to click it into place.

"Thanks," I say. "I um . . . I guess I forgot about that too." Now it's my turn to cringe. "Oh my God, I didn't mean—I'm sorry, I don't . . . this is . . ."

"Awkward?" Matt finishes for me.

"Yes," I say without thinking.

"I know. It is for me too." He takes a deep breath, then shakes his head. "I don't really know how to do this, Liv. I don't know what's okay, or how to act, or what to say."

"I don't either."

"But I want to try."

"I do too," I say.

He nods, and he looks at me for a moment with an expression that's both hopeful and sad, like he's searching for the girl he used to know and love, but isn't sure he'll be able to find her again.

I'm not sure either, but in this moment, I want to be that girl. I want to find her just as much as he does, so I reach out my hand and take his in mine. "So let's try. Take me somewhere we like to go."

"Are you hungry?" he asks.

"Yes," I lie.

"Okay," he says, and he puts the truck in drive. "That makes it easy."

A few minutes later we walk through the door of the Good Life, a café on the water that Matt says is my favorite.

The hostess gasps when she sees us and comes around from behind the podium. Hugs us both. "You two . . ." She shakes her head like she doesn't know what to say. "I'm just so glad you're okay."

Behind her, a few people turn and look at us. Some lean into each other and whisper.

I try to pretend like I don't notice.

"Thanks," Matt says, shifting uncomfortably.

When I don't say anything, it gets a little awkward.

"Well," she says with a smile. "Let's find you a table." She starts to lead us back to the empty one near the window, but when people look up and watch us, she stops. "You know, it's really nice on the patio. Would you rather sit out there today?"

I nod, wondering if I should know any of the people who all seem to be staring at us.

"That'd be great," Matt says. "Thank you."

Once we're seated outside, on the empty patio, in the sun and salty fresh air, I feel like I can breathe a little easier.

Across the table, Matt still looks a little tense, and I don't know if it's because of the people in the restaurant, or if it's being here, alone with me.

I try to put him at ease. "So, is this what our *first* first date was like?"

He laughs. "A little, I guess."

"How?"

"I was nervous. I'm pretty sure you were too."

I nod. "How did it go?" I don't say that Paige told me the story already. I want to hear how he remembers it.

Matt takes a drink of the water the busboy brought when we were seated. "Um, let's see," he says, leaning back in his chair a little. "I picked you up at your house. Before you came downstairs, your dad gave me the world's scariest pre-date 'talk,' in his uniform, with his hand resting on his gun." He laughs softly.

"I was nervous, so I didn't eat anything. You ate a whole plate of lasagna while I talked and tried not to fidget." He laughs at this. "I mean, it was *a lot* of lasagna. I'd never seen a girl eat that much. That sealed the deal right there, really."

I try not to laugh. "Nervous eating, maybe?"

He shakes his head. "No. You just eat a lot. Always have."

Now I can't help but laugh. I know this is true. It's a running joke in my family. "Fair enough. What else . . . ?"

"After that, we went for a walk on the pier, and I tried

to impress you by telling you all the stories I could remember about the constellations." He smiles. "Pretty sure I had them all mixed up, but you didn't seem to notice."

"And then?" I ask.

"And then I took you home."

"Did we kiss?" I ask, even though I know the answer.

He shakes his head. Looks down at the table.

"Why not?"

He brings his eyes back up to meet mine. "I liked you too much to try that night. I didn't want to rush anything."

He looks out over the water, and in the tiny moment before he looks back at me, I feel something besides just nervous, and I hope Paige was right. Maybe it's a spark. Maybe whatever we had is still here, hidden in all that emptiness.

"What else do you wanna know?" he asks when he looks back at me. "Ask me anything."

I nod, and try to feel braver than I do. "When *was* our first kiss?" My cheeks feel hot almost instantaneously. I try not to look at his lips. Lips that I've kissed who knows how many times.

"I was hoping you'd ask me that," he says.

"Why?"

"Because it's one of my favorite stories."

"Why?" I feel like a kid asking over and over, but now I'm even more curious to hear it from him. Maybe there's something Paige left out that he remembers.

A slow smile spreads over his face. "Because *you* kissed *me*."

He puts a hand up, like I might argue.

"And you always say it was the other way around, but it's true. You kissed me the first time. At Paige's house. We were all working on a project, and the power went out, and you asked me to go outside with you to see if it was the whole neighborhood." He pauses, and looks right at me with those blue eyes of his, and smiles. "The entire town was dark, and it was freezing out, but you asked me to tell you about Cassiopeia again. And I started to, but then you got a little closer, and you turned and stood on your tiptoes, and you kissed me right there, on her front porch."

"That's not how Paige told it," I say.

"That's not how you tell it either, but that's how it happened." He smiles. "It was a bold move."

I want to look away, but I keep my eyes on him, trying to picture it. Trying to picture myself doing something like that. "Did you . . . kiss me *back* at least?"

He laughs, looks down at the straw wrapper he's twirling between his fingers. "Yeah. I did." His eyes focus on something in the space between us, like he can see us standing there in his memory, and I wish, more than anything, that I could too.

"You were shivering," he says, looking up. "But your lips were warm." He pauses. Remembers something else.

"They tasted like cinnamon gum and that vanilla lip gloss you used to always wear."

As soon as he says it, I can see the little round tin of lip gloss with the vanilla ice cream cone on the lid. I gasp.

Matt raises hopeful eyebrows. "Liv? Did you—do you . . . ?"

He doesn't say the word *remember,* but I know that's what he's hoping. I wish I could tell him that I do.

I shake my head. "No, I . . . I mean I remember it from before. I've used that lip gloss ever since middle school. It's my favorite."

"Mine too," he says.

He looks at me now, and his smile fades the tiniest bit, and neither one of us knows what comes next. The quiet between us is so full with the things we don't know how to say—that this is sad, and strange, and uncomfortable all at the same time.

"So," I say, trying to get us back on track. "Apparently I have a summer job I'm going back to in a couple of days. Working at the Fuel Dock, with Sam?"

Matt smiles. "Yep. You actually really like that place— the boats, and all the different vacation people."

"Do you work too?"

"Yeah. At the pool. I lifeguard and teach swim lessons."

"And then what?"

"What do you mean?"

"After summer," I say. "Are you going away somewhere to school?"

Matt looks taken aback. "Um . . ." He shifts in his chair, clears his throat. "*We* are—or were—going together." He looks at me now. "To Cal Poly?"

Before I can answer, the waitress appears to take our orders.

"I heard you two sweeties were here," she says, her voice warm and familiar, like she knows us. She puts a gentle hand on my shoulder. "It's so good to see you're okay—we were all so worried about you, I mean—that was such an ordeal you went through. It must've been just terrifying."

I don't tell her that I don't remember it. Or her.

She brings her other hand to her chest and looks at Matt. "And to have it captured on video like that. Absolutely horrifying."

"I . . ." I have no idea how to respond to this.

Matt clears his throat and shifts in his seat again, and she glances at him. "I'm sorry, hon. Anyway. What can I getcha today? The usual?"

He orders a burger without looking at the menu.

She looks at me. "Vegwich and a side of fries with ranch?"

"Yeah. Sure." I try to smile.

"You got it," she says, then grabs our menus and goes back

inside like she didn't just make things hugely uncomfortable.

We both exhale and look at each other, but neither one of us says anything for a long moment. Then Matt does.

"So," he says, "fast-forward to the accident, I guess."

"I—we don't have to talk about that right now." I want to go back to hearing happy stories of us.

He looks at me, his mouth tight. "You've seen it, haven't you? The video."

I nod, and the images unfold in my mind. Matt, being pulled onto the boat. Matt, yelling and panicking while Walker pulled me in and then started CPR. Matt, trying to pull him off me. And the two of them—fighting.

"I panicked," Matt says, like he can read my mind. "I panicked when I couldn't get you out, and then when he did." He looks down at his hands again. "And I panicked when he started pumping on your chest." He swallows hard. "I could hear your ribs breaking, Liv. It was the worst thing I've ever heard, and I . . . I freaked out. I tried to make him stop because I thought he was hurting you. That's why I went after him like that." He pauses, and we're both quiet. "I'm sorry," he says quietly. "I just need you to know what happened, because I hate the way it looks—like I . . ."

He shakes his head. "I don't know. Like I could've done more. Or like I tried to stop him from helping you."

He looks at me with sad eyes, and I can see the guilt everywhere in him—from his eyes, to the way his mouth is set, to the slump of his shoulders and the twisting of his hands. And what I feel for him in this moment is empathy.

I reach both of my hands across the table and take his, which are tense, almost fists. "It's okay. You don't have anything to be sorry about. You told him I was still down there. You helped him pull me onto the boat."

His hands are still tense in mine, and he shakes his head, avoiding my eyes.

"Hey," I say, more forcefully now. "You did everything you could. And I'm okay. I'm here, and I'm okay, and we'll figure this out together." Even as I say the words, I feel distant from them. Like I'm playing the part of myself. But I really do want to help him, and it seems to be what he needs to hear, because his hands relax the tiniest bit.

He looks down at the table for a moment, and when he brings his eyes back to mine, it's hard to tell what I see there.

"There's . . . there's something I need to ask you," he says finally.

"Okay," I say. Tentative, because his tone is so serious.

"And you can say no. I'll understand." He runs a nervous hand through his hair and looks at me. "There's this reporter who's been calling me. She keeps asking for an interview, and . . ." He pauses, takes a deep breath. "She says it'd be good for everyone to see us together—to let them know that we're both okay."

I think of the huge bouquet and the card that's now buried deep in my desk drawer, and I'm sure it's from the same reporter, because she mentioned talking to him and Walker.

"And," he says, his hands still holding mine, "she thinks it'd be a good chance for me to set things straight about what happened on that video, and . . ." He pauses. "I think she might be right."

I don't say anything—not at first, because I'm turning the possibility over in my mind. I wouldn't be able to answer any questions about the accident—or the last few years leading up to it. And I'm not sure I'm ready for anyone watching to know that.

"I'm sorry," Matt says quickly. "I shouldn't have asked. Forget I did, okay?"

"No, it's just . . . I don't know." Another thought occurs to me. "Would Walker James be there too?" I ask. I can't keep the hopeful note out of my voice, and it makes me feel immediately guilty.

Matt doesn't seem to notice. "I don't know," he says. "She was trying to get him too, but I kinda doubt it. I heard he left town."

I think about what she *did* say in her note. That she'd talked to them both and they'd been open to it. Maybe Matt just doesn't know that. Maybe he's just assuming Walker wouldn't agree to an interview. But if there's a chance that he *could* be there, I wouldn't have to just hope to run into him. I could see him, face-to-face, and thank him for what he did. This possibility makes me want to say yes, but the thought of going on the news in front of the cameras as an amnesiac accident victim makes me feel a little queasy.

"I . . ." I look at Matt. "Can I think about it?"

"Of course. Yeah. I don't want to make you feel like you have to, or force you into anything you don't want to do."

"You're not," I say. "It's just, I don't know if I want to talk about this in an interview. I mean, about me, how I can't remember anything. I don't know if I want everybody to know that."

Matt starts to answer, but the waitress shows up at our table just then, carrying a plate in each hand. She sets Matt's burger in front of him and then turns to me and smiles.

"Here you go, sweetheart. Veggie burger, extra lettuce, no sauce, add avo. Just like you like it."

"Thank you," I say, looking at what is apparently my usual. It strikes me then that maybe nobody would have to know. She was none the wiser, just like Chloe, and the kids on the dock. None of them had any idea how much of me is missing, and what they don't see they just fill in with their own assumptions.

"I'm sorry," Matt says, as soon as the waitress walks away. "I shouldn't have asked."

"No, it's okay." I look at him now. "I think I actually

would like to do it. She left me her number in a card. I can call when I get home."

"Really?" He reaches across the table and takes my hands. "You would do that for me?"

"Of course," I say. And though I feel a twinge of guilt, I let him assume his own reasons why.

FIFTEEN

THROUGHOUT THE REST of our dinner, I get to hear Matt's version of us, which is sweet and funny. He answers all my questions but doesn't overwhelm me with stories I don't know to ask about. He pokes fun at himself, but is kind about me. By the time we finish, I can see what drew me to him, even if I don't entirely feel it yet. Sparks are probably too much to expect at this point, anyway.

We step out onto the boardwalk, the crowd thinning in the warm evening light, and Matt looks at me. "Where to next? Dessert? It's still early."

This jogs something in my mind. "What time is it?"

He checks his phone. "Quarter to six."

"Can we stop by the camera shop real quick? I dropped

some film off earlier, and she said it'd be finished by closing."

"Sure," Matt says. He looks amused. "Actual film? You have a camera that uses actual film?"

"Yes," I say, and I stop walking. Matt didn't know about me taking pictures either. It makes me nervous, about what I'd been taking pictures of. "It's . . . actually, you know what? We don't need to go right now. They close at six, and I can come back tomorrow."

He gives me a funny look. "It's no problem. It's right around the corner."

"No, it's okay. I'll just come back."

"But we're here right now. Come on. We can make it." He reaches for my hand with that smile, and those dimples, and against my better judgment, I take his hand, and in a few moments he's opening the door to the shop.

The bells jingle.

"Sorry, we're closing," a voice calls from behind the printing machine.

"Okay," I answer, taking it as an excuse to turn right back around and come back tomorrow, by myself.

Matt stops me. "We just have some pictures to pick up, that's all."

I hear a sigh from behind the machine, and then a girl comes out. "Of course. It's no problem at all, why would it matter that we're closing, it's just a—Liv?"

She says my name at the same time I realize it's her.

"Jules?"

"Hey," Matt says. "I didn't know you worked here."

She doesn't answer him, and she doesn't take her eyes off me. I search them for the familiarity that I remember, half expecting her to come around the counter and hug me like Chloe did, but she doesn't.

"Wow. I'm glad you're okay," she says finally. "That video was—that was pretty crazy."

I feel Matt tense at this.

"Yeah, we're okay," I say, trying not to be shocked at how different she looks—even from this year's yearbook photos. Her hair is a cut short and dyed a shocking shade of red, and there's a tiny stud in her nose. "How . . . how are you?"

I sound awkward, stiff, I know it. But I can't help it. I'm starting to freak out. I wasn't expecting to see her here, and I still don't know what happened with us, and she doesn't know I don't know, and I can't start asking about all this with Matt standing right here while we're waiting for pictures I took but didn't tell anyone about.

"I'm good," she says, keeping her eyes on mine. "Fine."

We're all quiet a moment, and I try to read what's there.

"So . . ." Matt starts.

"Right. Your pictures. Lemme grab 'em."

She goes in the back, and he turns to me. "You okay? You seem . . ."

"I'm fine. Just tired. I think I need to go home after this."

"Sure, of course."

Jules comes back out carrying the envelope of photos and hands it to me. It's thinner than I expect when I take it.

"Sorry," she says, "there were only a few that printed from that roll. The rest was blank."

"It's okay. I expected that."

She rings me up, and I pay.

"Thank you," I say. And then, "It's good to see you."

Her face softens the tiniest bit, and she almost smiles. "You too, Liv. Take care."

And that's it. Matt and I leave, and she flips the sign in the window to Closed, and seeing her for the first time is over. It happened that quickly, without me having a chance to ask about what happened with us. After a few steps, I steal a glance over my shoulder, half expecting her to still be in the window, but it's empty.

"So are you gonna look at those?" Matt asks as he drives.

I'm looking out my window, holding in tears and replaying the tiny interaction with my former best friend, trying to figure out how things could've possibly changed so much between us, and hoping that it wasn't something I did.

"Liv?"

"What? Oh." I glance down at the envelope in my lap, and then at Matt. "No, they're not anything. Just something for my mom."

I wince inwardly at the lie, but I can't look at these pictures right now, with Matt. Not when I'd been keeping it from him that I'd even taken them.

A knot starts to form in my stomach, and by the time we pull into my driveway, I have to tell myself to breathe, and smile, and talk. I thank him for taking me out, and we stand there awkwardly at the door for a second.

"So . . . I'll call you tomorrow?"

I nod. "Sounds good."

"And you'll call Dana Whitmore?"

"Yes."

"Okay. Thank you." He steps closer and looks me in the eye. "Good night, Liv."

"Good night," I say, and he leans forward and places the softest kiss on my forehead. It's sweet, almost chaste, but I feel it there as I walk through the door into the living room. I feel it there when my parents stop me in the living room and ask too many questions about my day, and I feel it all the way up the stairs and into my room.

It isn't until I finally sit down at my desk with the envelope and pull the pictures out that I feel something else entirely.

Surprise.

I flip past the shots I know—from the harbor, the two from the beach, the blurry one of me in my room, and the shot of Sam and Paige mugging next to each other on my bed.

There are three left after that. The first is of a sunset over the ocean. Nothing spectacular. The next one is of what looks like a natural pool in the rocks. It's taken from above, and the water in the pool is so clear and blue it almost doesn't look real.

The last one is a shot of me, and it's recent.

My hair is wild, blowing around me in the wind, and lit up golden brown by the sun that gives the whole shot a warm glow. I'm looking almost beyond the camera, and I can tell I'm laughing. I look at ease, and so happy.

I spread the last three photos out on my desk and examine each one for any detail that could be a magical puzzle piece—the thing that clicks and brings something back to me. But nothing stands out. I don't feel disappointed, exactly. Just more confused. I hadn't expected a shot of myself. I'd always felt more comfortable behind the lens than in front of it, so it's strange to me that I look so relaxed in this picture. Strange that I would've let someone else take a picture of me with my camera.

I look at it again, at the warm glow, and the smile on my face, and now, if I remember just one thing, out of everything I've forgotten, I wish it could be to know who took this photo. I tuck it, along with the others, into the thin frame of my chalkboard wall and look at them against the backdrop of all the other things I don't understand.

I read it all, over and over, go back to the pictures again and again, but it doesn't matter. Even with all this right in front of me, I'm still locked outside myself.

SIXTEEN

THE NEXT MORNING, I wait until I hear both of my parents get up and leave for the walk I've learned they now take every Saturday. After they're gone, I dress in my own workout clothes so that if Sam's still here, I can leave under the pretense of going for my own walk. I could use a little moving, breathing, thinking time to myself, anyway. Before I leave, I grab my three pictures and tuck them into the pocket of my hoodie.

As soon as I open my bedroom door, I know without question that Sam's here still because I smell bacon cooking. Another thing that hasn't changed. Ever since we were kids—and apparently, still—Sam has bacon for breakfast every Saturday. No eggs, or toast, or even juice. Just bacon. Lots of it.

"Ah," he says when I walk into the kitchen. "I knew the smell would do the trick. Even made some extra for you. And you have to try it, because you probably don't remember, but I've basically perfected my method."

I glance at the stovetop, expecting to see the big bacon pan he got for Christmas when he was twelve and I was ten, but it's not there. His As Seen on TV Microwave Magic Bacon Cooker from the next year isn't around either. He is, however, wearing an apron that looks like a giant slice of bacon. Apparently from a Christmas I don't recall.

"Oven bacon," he says, movie announcer–style. "Allows for the maximum number of strips to be done at one time, uniform cooking, and perfect balance of crispy and chewy. Plus, there's no mess for Mom to get mad at me about." He turns on the oven light and peers through the window, then checks the egg timer we've had as long as I can remember. "Two more minutes."

He looks back at me, then notices my workout clothes. "Wait, you're not leaving before breakfast, are you? It's Faturday. We eat a ridiculous amount of bacon and then lie around for a while wishing we didn't. Remember?" The corner of his mouth twitches, and he tries not to smile.

"Actually, I do," I say. I reach for a banana from the fruit bowl. "But I don't think I do that anymore. You know, with the whole vegetarian thing?"

He gives me a look. "Stop it with that already." He reaches over and takes the banana from me. Puts it back in the fruit bowl. "Now you're just being crazy. You realize you can do what you want to do, right? You don't just have to do what everybody says you did before."

"Didn't you just tell me what I did before?"

Sam thinks about it for a moment. "Well, yeah, technically, but that's different. I was just reminding you of something you already like and remember. Not telling you something that you don't. Either way," he says with a smile, "it is my very strong recommendation that you try the bacon."

It does smell good, and I *am* hungry after not eating much dinner last night. And Sam is, well, Sam. He's hard to say no to.

"Fine. I'll have a piece," I say, sitting down at the kitchen island. "Just to see if you really have perfected your method."

"Oh, I have." He raises an eyebrow and smiles like he always has, with all the confidence in the world. "Just you wait."

It's quiet a moment. I run my fingers over the swirls in the granite of the countertop. He checks his bacon again. The timer ticks away from its spot on the counter between us.

"Sam?"

"Yeah?"

"Can I ask you a question?"

"Sure, yeah, of course." He leans against the counter and crosses his arms over his bacon apron, trying to look casual, but it makes him look nervous. "Anything. Ask away."

I hesitate. Find a dark vein in the granite and follow it to its end with my finger, wondering if we kept in touch once he went to school. Or if I told him anything. It's not inconceivable. Last I remember, we were close enough for me to ask him what he thought about the boy I had a crush on in eighth grade and he actually gave me decent advice. The fact that there's a chance I still did that sort of thing makes me brave enough to ask.

"Did we . . . did we talk much this last year? I mean, since you went to school?"

He shrugs. "Not too much. We texted sometimes." He grins. "And there were a few 'I Love You, Man' phone calls that I'm pretty sure were wine cooler–fueled."

I choose to ignore that part, as I still can't picture drinking, or chancing the trouble I'd get in with our dad for that. "I called you?"

"Not a lot. But sometimes. Because I'm awesome and you love me so much."

"Did I talk about Matt a lot?"

"Probably. I don't know, it was pretty late the few times you called. You woke me up, and I just mumbled 'uh-huh' until you were done talking and ready to hang up."

"Did I ever mention anyone else?"

Sam goes still, and there's a long moment before he answers my question. "You mean like other people besides him? In general? Yeah, probably. I mean, most of us don't just talk about one person."

"I mean, did I ever mention any other guys? That kind of someone else."

"Nope. Not that I remember." He turns, opens the oven, and pulls the pan of bacon out even though there's still a minute left on the timer, then makes himself busy fanning the steam away. Not looking at me.

My brother has always been a terrible liar.

"What did I say?" I ask.

He grabs a pair of tongs and starts transferring the slices of bacon to the paper towel–lined plate he has ready on the counter. "Nothing."

"Sam."

He looks at me now. "Not much." He fidgets with the tongs in his hand. "I didn't even know what you were talk-ing about at first."

"What do you mean? What did I say?"

Sam takes a deep breath and lets it out in a big sigh.

"Just . . ." He pauses, and I can see he doesn't want to tell me. "Just that you'd kinda started hanging out with someone. A guy."

"And?" I have a sinking feeling that there's more. Maybe a lot more, that I might not want to know about myself.

Sam's face confirms it. He takes another deep breath. "And that you and Matt were . . . drifting a little."

"And you didn't think this was important to *tell* me? Oh my God, Sam, why didn't you *say* anything?"

"I . . . you just mentioned it once. And then the next time we talked, it was all back to Matt again, so I . . ."

He looks helpless standing there in his bacon apron, so helpless that if I wasn't so angry, I might actually feel sorry for him. But I don't—not in this moment. All I feel is anger.

"You what? Oh wait, you lied to me, is what."

"I didn't *lie*, I just—"

"Didn't tell me the truth, which is basically the same thing." I get up to leave, but I don't even know where I would go.

"Stop. Liv, c'mon. I was trying to make things easier for you."

"How does *not* telling me something like that make things *easier*?" I'm yelling now and I don't even care. "How does telling me how much I love my boyfriend I can't even remember make anything *easier*? Especially when it's not even *true*!"

"But you do love him—or you did. Shit." He frowns. "It's complicated. And it just seemed better that way."

"Lying to me? How was that better?"

"I told you, I didn't lie," he says quietly.

"No. You didn't. You just decided it would be better for me not to know something I confided in you."

"I honestly didn't think it was that important." He sits down on the stool next to me. Rubs his forehead. "I'm sorry. It was just—Matt's a good guy, and you two were good together, and . . ." He shakes his head. "I'm sorry, Liv. I was just trying to make it easier for you because whatever else you were doing—and trying to hide—was making things hard for you."

"Did I say who?" I ask quietly.

"No."

"Do Mom and Dad know about this too? Or Matt? Or Paige? Is *everyone* in on this?" The thought of them all keeping a secret like this from me makes me want to throw something, break something, anything.

"No," Sam says firmly. "They're not. You told me, and I kept my mouth shut because that's what I do."

"Apparently. You kept my own secret from me."

"I was trying to protect you."

"From what? *Myself?*"

"No," Sam says so calmly I want to punch him. "From everything you would've screwed up if you'd let it go anywhere. You and Matt are serious. You have plans. You're even going to the same freakin' college."

"Am I? I don't see how that's possible, seeing as I don't

remember high school." It's not until I say it that I realize something I can't believe I haven't thought of until now. I didn't just lose my past. I've lost my future too. Or whatever future it was that past me had all planned out.

Sam waves a dismissive hand. "It'll come back."

"What if it doesn't?"

He thinks for a moment. "Then you'll figure out something else. Honestly? I was surprised you were gonna do the whole volleyball, business major thing to begin with. You stopped liking volleyball years ago, and I never figured you for business school. You were never into that. Not the way you were into other stuff."

"Like what?" I ask.

He shrugs. "I don't know, artsy stuff. Taking pictures."

I reach for my pocket and pull out the three pictures. Lay them on the counter between us. He looks at them, then at me for some sort of explanation.

"These were on my camera," I say. "I think I was taking pictures again and not telling anyone, but I don't know why, and I don't know where or when these were taken."

Sam picks up the one of the pool, in the rocky cove. "Well, this is on Vista Island, but it's hard to access. You'd have to take a kayak or a boat there. Maybe you and Matt went out there? He was asking me about it last time I was home."

We're both quiet a moment, then Sam clears his throat.

Points at the one of me. "That's a nice one of you."

I look at him, surprised.

"What? It is. You look really happy."

I'm still mad at him, I am. But I look at my brother then, and I feel like I want to hug him. For knowing me probably better than anyone else, and for being here now.

"Here," he says, "have some bacon. It'll give you clarity. Offer a whole new perspective on life."

"You're ridiculous."

"I think you mean ridiculously awesome."

"No, that's not what I meant."

"It will be after you taste this. Come on. Take the bacon."

I laugh and look at the now-cold strip of bacon he holds between us like an olive branch. And even though I'm still mad at him for not telling me the truth about me, I take it. And when I bite into it, it's worth it. It really is the best bacon he's ever made, though I don't give him the satisfaction of me saying that out loud.

We eat the rest in silent appreciation, and when it's all gone, I help Sam clean up the kitchen.

"So are we cool?" he asks as he closes the dishwasher. "Because you're on the schedule for Monday, and I need to know that you're going to take me seriously as your boss. Like, super seriously."

I look at him standing there in his bacon apron, his morning hair still sticking up in every direction.

"Of course. I just need to you cover with me for Mom and Dad tomorrow afternoon."

"For what?"

I shake my head. "Just something I need to do, that I know they'd say no to."

"Well, that narrows it down. Sure. Yeah. No questions asked."

I cross the kitchen and give him a big hug. "Thank you, you weirdo."

He puts his arms around me for an awkward half a second, then steps back. "That's boss weirdo to you."

SEVENTEEN

THE NEXT AFTERNOON, Matt picks me up because my car is still at the bottom of the bay—and because I don't know how to drive. He opens the passenger door and helps me up into the truck. This time, I remember about the seat belt, and pull it slowly across my lap until I can click it. This makes him smile, but I can tell he's nervous. I am too. Dana Whitmore had been happy to take my call, and even happier to schedule an interview ASAP, before I had to go back to work.

I don't mention to Matt that I didn't ask my parents if I could do this or tell them where we're headed. I know what their answer would've been, and by the time they see it, it'll be too late. I'll face the consequences then. I don't know if this is something I would've ever done before, but it's something I feel like I need to do now—for Matt, and, if I'm being honest, for me too. Dana Whitmore had said she'd do her best to get Walker to show, and if there's any chance he does, I want to be there.

I look over at Matt as he drives. He's dressed in a striped collared shirt and a dark tie, his blond hair combed neatly, face freshly shaven. He's definitely good-looking in that classic, clean-cut kind of way. And it's kind of endearing how he keeps glancing over and smiling nervously. I try to embrace these thoughts, try to remind myself that he's my boyfriend, and we love each other, and whatever I'd said to my brother had probably blown over, like he said. So now, if I just keep playing the part, the rest will come naturally. I hope, anyway.

"You look nice," I say, reaching across the seat and brushing his shoulder with my hand.

He glances down at my touch and smiles. "Thanks. First time Homecoming clothes are good for more than one night."

"So we don't dress up much?"

He looks at me. "Not really. For special occasions, mostly."

"I assume we went to all the dances? Danced? Had fun?" I run my eyes over his shirt and tie again, trying to summon even a flash of this.

He smiles. "Yeah." It's quiet for a few seconds, then he looks at me again. "We're good, dancing together. People watch when we do."

This makes me laugh. "That's probably because I can't dance. I *do* remember that much." And I do. In seventh grade, I hit a growth spurt that rendered me tall, gangly, and comically uncoordinated.

"That's not true," Matt says. Then he laughs. "I mean, it's taken years of practice, but you've gotten a lot better."

"So you're saying I can dance now?"

He nods. "Oh yeah."

"I don't believe you."

"Then I'll just have to show you one of these days," he says with a smile.

"Okay," I say. "Deal."

We fall back into silence, and I try to think of something else to talk about before the relative ease of it slips into awkwardness.

Matt beats me to it. "You look nice too," he says. "Is that a new dress? I don't recognize it."

I look down at the dress I'm wearing, one of about twenty that I pulled out of my closet, tried on, and finally settled on. "Well, that makes two of us, because I have no idea."

For whatever reason, this strikes me as funny rather than strange or sad, like most other things have, and it makes me laugh, which still hurts. But I'm glad because Matt starts laughing too, and by the time we pull into the lot of our local news studio, it feels like a start of some sort. A turning point, maybe, that we can laugh together at a tiny part of our situation.

I can feel us both relax a little, but that lasts only until he parks and shuts off the truck. We both look out the windshield at the news station building in front of us, but neither of us makes a move to get out.

Matt looks at me. "Are you sure you want to do this? I don't—I hope I didn't pressure you into it. Especially if you're not ready."

"You didn't," I say. "She contacted me too, and I thought about it, and I decided I want to. I really do." I pause. "The only thing is, I don't . . ."

His eyes run over my face, searching for what I'm trying to say as I try to figure out how to say it, but he doesn't push. He gives me time to find it.

"I just really don't want to talk about my memory loss," I say.

He nods.

"I mean, I know it's normal not to remember the accident, but I don't want people to know about the rest because . . . I don't want the whole story to turn into that, and have to answer a whole bunch of questions about it."

"Of course. I won't mention it."

"Thank you," I say. "I want this to be about us. And moving forward."

The words sound like someone else's in my ears, but this is what I've decided moving forward is for me right now.

Matt's eyes soften, and he takes a deep breath and lets it out slowly. "Thank you, Liv," he says, and he leans into me, close. Inside, I tell myself it's okay if he kisses me. He's my boyfriend, and we've probably kissed thousands of times. Still, I feel myself tense up.

Again, it's like he can read my mind. Or my body language. He stops in the middle of the space between us and gives me a smile that's more sad than anything else. Leans back in his seat. We're both quiet, and neither one of us knows what to say or how to acknowledge the strangeness of the moment.

"Liv," he says quietly. "Whatever happens with this—with us, I want you to know I love you."

I fight the urge to look away. "I . . ."

"You don't need to say it back," he says quickly. "I just . . . need you to know that."

I nod, relieved. And surprised. This may be harder than I thought.

We get out and walk around to the front of his truck, and he takes my hand in his, and when we walk into the studio, I remind myself that it's as a couple who've been together for over two years, who went through something traumatic together, and who should be closer and stronger because of it.

As soon as we walk through the door, we're greeted by a young guy in a headset who ushers us down a hallway to a room where he asks us to wait for Dana Whitmore. No sooner does he leave than she walks through the door wearing a jacket, skirt, and heels that push the definition of professional.

"Hello, you two!" She says, arms outstretched as she walks to the couch we're sitting on, huge TV smile plastered to her heavily made-up face. Her teeth are the most brilliant shade of white I've ever seen, and it takes me a moment to realize that Matt has greeted her already and that I should too.

I reach a hand out, but she takes a step past it and envelops me with a hug and perfume that smells exactly how she looks. "And Liv," she says, pulling me back by my shoulders like my mom would, which seems odd given that she can't be that much older than me. "How *are* you?"

She asks it like it's a huge question—one you'd end with multiple question marks if you were writing it.

"I'm good," I say, taking the tiniest step back to put a little distance between us. She's a lot.

She takes the hint, steps back too, and shifts into business mode. "Well, thank you both, so much, for agreeing to come in. This was such a big local story, but we're still getting inquiries from all over the country—people wanting to know how you two are doing, so this is a great chance to let them know that you're okay—heroics, and healing, and human triumph, and all." She smiles again. "Can I get you anything before we go on? Water? Soda? Restroom? We've got a couple minutes."

Matt and I both shake our heads. "No thanks," I say.

She claps her hands. "Okay then. Let's head to the studio. We'll get you all set up and then get started."

She leads us back down the same hall to a door that opens up into the studio. There is a brightly lit stage with a chair and a small couch on it, surrounded by multiple large cameras. My stomach does a flip-flop as she leads us to the couch and gestures for Matt and me to sit.

It's just us. There's no sign of Walker.

I try not to look disappointed as the same young guy appears out of nowhere with two mics—one that he clips to Matt's shirt, and another that he hands to me, with instructions to clip it to my dress. Someone swings a light our way, momentarily blinding us. I flinch and blink, and it moves away. Dana sits down across from us and smooths her dress. Clips on her own mic. A girl comes by with a big makeup brush and adds another layer to her face.

Dana smiles at us again. "Just so you know, this isn't live. It'll go up as an edited segment tomorrow or the next day, so if you stumble over an answer, don't worry. Just try to relax and tell your story, okay?" She punctuates the question with another wide smile, sits up impossibly straight in her chair, and before Matt or I can respond, the bright light beams on us again and the young guy behind the camera is counting down.

Dana angles herself toward the camera, her face now serious. "Thank you, Mark. And now I have a very special report for you. Over two weeks ago, Pelican Bay witnessed an accident that could have been one of the worst tragedies this town has seen when the driver of an eighteen-wheeler lost control of his truck and struck a car carrying two teenage passengers, sending them off the Carson Bridge and into the bay. But today I'm here with Matt Turner and Olivia Jordan, the two teens who miraculously survived this accident." Now she looks at us. "Matt, Olivia, thank you so much for being here. I know you've been through a lot in these past few weeks."

She pauses, and for a moment I'm not sure if I'm supposed to answer, but then she picks right back up. "So can you tell us about what happened that night—before your car was hit?"

She's looking at me, and all of a sudden I don't know what I was thinking saying yes to this, because I have no idea how to answer. I try not to panic, try to search through what I've been told and what I've seen and read, for the basics, but all I can think of is that I don't want her or anyone watching to know that I don't remember. That I'm still so broken.

I swallow. "I . . ." I feel my cheeks get hot, and the heavy weight of the emptiness in my mind.

"We were coming home from a friend's house on Farris Island," Matt says, rescuing me.

"It was a party, wasn't it?" Dana Whitmore asks.

There's a beat before Matt answers again. "Yes."

"Was there drinking going on at the party?"

"Um . . . I don't see what that has to do with the accident," Matt says, his brows drawn together.

"Were *you* drinking that night?"

Matt shifts in his seat, and I wonder if he was—or if he even does. I have no idea. Maybe that's what he'd meant the other day, about people saying things. Maybe that's why he feels so guilty. But he shouldn't, even if he was drinking. I was the one driving.

"I . . ." Matt looks helpless.

I want to save him, and somehow that gives me the voice to speak up, even though I don't know the truth.

"No, we weren't," I say firmly. "And that's irrelevant anyway. The accident happened because the truck hit us from behind."

I see Matt's shoulders relax the tiniest bit, but he doesn't chance a thank-you glance at me.

Dana seems to accept my answer. "Okay, so let's talk about what that was like, when the truck hit you. Did you see it coming? Did you try to react?"

She's looking at me again, and again I don't know the answer. I don't have an answer. "I don't remember," I say quietly.

Matt puts a hand on my knee and squeezes gently. "We both saw the lights in the rearview. They were too bright and too close all of a sudden. She didn't have a chance to react, because right after that it hit us."

"And it sent you over?"

Matt answers again. "Not right away. It pushed us up and over the guardrail, and there was a second where the car kind of just sat there."

Dana Whitmore looks at me. "That must have been terrifying. Did you try to get out?"

Matt saves me again. "We didn't have time. Because then it tipped and we were falling. The car hit the water and glass exploded. Then the water came pouring in through all the windows."

Dana Whitmore is shaking her head. "So what were you thinking at this point?"

"That we were gonna die if we didn't get out." Matt falls quiet, looks down at his lap.

"And what happened next?" Dana asks, softening her tone a little.

Matt looks up at her, his hands twisting in his lap. "We started to sink. Fast. And water and airbags were everywhere, and I was trying not to panic, but I couldn't even see her."

He looks in my direction, but it's like he's seeing that night. Like he's remembering. And for the first time since the accident, I'm glad I don't remember.

"I didn't know if she was alive," he continues. "But I knew we needed to get out because we were sinking so fast." He shakes his head. "I don't know how I did it—the water and the adrenaline woke me up, I guess. I was holding my breath, and pulling myself out, and then I was free, and I found her and tried to get her out, but I was running out of air."

"So you had to swim up to the surface?"

"I . . ."

Matt's hands are shaking. He looks at me with eyes so sorry I wish we could just get up and leave right this moment.

Dana waits, giving him time to answer. I can't handle seeing him this way. Now it's me who takes Matt's hand, and I hope the camera sees it.

"I didn't want to leave her down there."

"But you needed air," Dana fills in.

He takes a deep breath like he needs air now too, then nods. "Yeah. I swam up, and took a breath, and dove back down. I could see the headlights, so I followed them. And I got to her, but she was stuck in her seat belt like I was, and I couldn't get her out."

This is the first time I've heard the story in his words, with his details. I don't remember it, but I can see it like I do. The broken glass, the dark water pouring in through the windows. I can almost feel the burning in Matt's chest as he tried to hold his breath to get me out. The thought of it puts a lump in my throat, because for the first time since I've woken up I realize that the accident didn't just happen to me. This happened to both of us, and having the memory of it might be just as bad as not being able to remember what came before it.

"That must've been absolutely terrifying," Dana says sympathetically.

"Yeah." Matt glances at me and presses his lips together for a moment before he continues. "I knew she was gonna die if I couldn't get her out." He shakes his head. "I just wanted to get her out."

I put my other hand on top of his. Try to remind him that I did get out, and I'm here with him, and that we're here together.

Dana nods and turns to the camera. "It was at this time that Walker James, a nineteen-year-old fisherman, was coming into the harbor on a small boat. This footage was captured by an eyewitness."

Behind us, a short clip of the video appears. Matt doesn't look at it. He just stares straight ahead, but I can't help it. This I know, like it's a memory. The headlights in the water. Matt's waving arms, barely visible in the lights from the bridge. The boat slowing down.

I glance at Dana, who has one hand on her headset and the other over her ear, like she's trying to hear something over the hissing sound of the wind in the video. It stops, and the image of the boat freezes on the screen. Dana straightens up. Puts on that smile again, and looks at the camera.

"At this time I'd like to welcome Walker James, the young man who was on that boat, and whose heroic efforts saved the lives of these two teens that fateful night."

What happens next feels like it's in fast-forward and slow motion at the same time. Dana waits, her too-wide smile still in place, mascara-covered lashes blinking expectantly. Matt lets go of my hand. Sits up, ramrod straight, looking around. And I am frozen in place, heart pounding in my ears as Walker James steps out from the darkness behind the cameras, onto the stage with us.

EIGHTEEN

WALKER JAMES WEARS a beat-up pair of jeans, work boots, a faded T-shirt, and an almost-scowl on his unshaven face as he crosses the stage.

Dana stands and extends her hand. "Walker, welcome. Wow. Thank you so much for joining us on such short notice."

He gives her hand one shake and acknowledges her with a nod, but doesn't say anything. His expression says it all, though. He looks like he'd rather be anywhere but here. It makes me wonder why he's here at all.

I take a nervous breath, notice the familiar pinch in my ribs. And then the air goes right out of me, because in this moment I realize that the pain that I still feel is connected to Walker, who is standing right in front of me, and to what he did that night to save my life. I flash on the image of him, above my body on the boat deck, and my hands feel the tiniest bit shaky.

"Please, sit down," Dana is saying. She motions to the couch, and I realize the only place for him to sit is on the other side of me.

Walker's eyes flick to the empty space, and I scoot closer to Matt to make room. Matt stands so he can pass, and they shake hands, nodding at each other like guys do. And then it's my turn to greet him. I stand, not quite sure what to do. He looks like he doesn't know either, and our eyes catch, and I see the green of his. It's a moment that stretches out, tense, until Walker breaks it by extending his hand. I take it with my own, we shake, and meeting the person who saved my life is over in just a few seconds, too fast for me to even begin to process, and I want to slow it down because it's a moment I thought would be bigger somehow.

We all sit back down, and I swear the air feels different with Walker there. Charged. I can even see it in the deep breath Dana takes and the extra-wide smile she plasters on. She didn't mention this when we arrived, and I wonder if it was a surprise even to her. Either that or she intentionally didn't tell us he'd be here. I glance at Matt, wondering if he would've agreed to come on had he thought there was a chance Walker actually would show up.

He reaches for my hand again, and it brings me back to us, here and now. I take it and lean into him the tiniest bit, because all of a sudden I feel incredibly self-conscious sitting there in the middle of the couch between him and Walker, who has put himself as far away from me as possible.

Dana, who is watching us all very carefully, seems to take this as her cue.

"Walker, thank you so much for being with us today." She looks at me. "Olivia, there must be *so* much going through your mind right now. This is the first time since the accident that you've come face-to-face with the person who saved your life. What does that feel like?"

"I . . ." I look at Walker, then at Matt, then back at Dana. I have no idea how to answer this—not just because I can't pin down what I'm feeling, but because Matt's hand squeezes tighter around mine.

Walker clears his throat and speaks for the first time. "We both pulled her in."

Dana nods, but it's dismissive. "Yes, but I think it's safe to say that she wouldn't be here today if not for you. So let's go back to that night, back to the moment you knew something was wrong. You were coming in from a fishing run just after the accident, correct?"

Walker glances at me, then looks back at Dana. "Sure."

"What did you see?"

He takes a deep breath and lets it out in a puff. Sits back

against the couch and avoids making eye contact with any of us. "I saw the truck on the bridge. People all lined up, looking over. And then the lights underwater." He glances across me, at Matt. "I heard him yelling."

Dana turns to Matt. "At that point, you'd seen his boat coming in?"

"Yeah," Matt answers. His tone is curt. Tense. He knows what's coming next. We all do.

Dana turns back to Walker. "So you heard him yelling, and headed in that direction?"

"Yeah, I took the boat over and was trying to get him up on it, but he didn't want to go."

Dana nods, looking at Matt sympathetically. When she speaks, her voice is more serious. "Because Olivia was still stuck inside the car."

It's not a question, but Walker and Matt say yes from both sides of me.

"And that's when you jumped in?"

Walker nods.

"I don't think most people would've done that," Dana says. "Do you have any formal rescue training? Is that a part of working on a fishing crew?"

Walker looks irritated. "No."

"How did you know you'd be able to get to her? I mean, what about the depth of the water?"

Walker shrugs. "I didn't know. But the lights weren't that far from the shore, so I thought there was a chance."

"And there was, wasn't there? You were able to get to her," Dana says, like she's building up to a big moment.

"Yeah," Walker says, clearly not interested in giving it to her.

"What was that *like*?" she presses.

He takes another impatient deep breath, like he doesn't want to tell the story, or like he's had to tell it too many times, I can't tell which.

"Cold. Dark. But I could see her arms and her hair, floating in the light."

A chill runs through me at the image.

"I tried to get her out through the window, but her seat belt was stuck."

"Is that how you injured your arm?" Dana asks, motioning at him.

I look over at him and notice the bandage on one of his forearms.

"Yeah," he says with a shrug.

My chest squeezes. This happened to him too.

"So what happened next?" Dana asks.

"I had to come up for air. And I grabbed the knife out of my belt." He pauses. "Then I dove down again and cut the seat belt."

"And we all know what happened after that," Dana says, moving the story along. "We've all seen the chilling footage of this heroic rescue."

Perfectly on cue, the shaky footage unfreezes, and I brace myself, keenly aware of the studio cameras on me. It doesn't matter how many times I've seen it, it still puts a knot in my stomach. I try to keep my expression neutral as we watch Walker, swimming with my body to the boat, where he and Matt drag me up onto the deck, and then Matt paces frantically.

I feel Matt's hand tighten around mine again. I squeeze back and try to keep my breathing even.

On the other side of me, Walker shifts again and looks away from the screen, and for a second I have the impulse to reach my other hand out to him because it seems like it's hard for him to watch too.

But then on the screen, he rips my shirt open and starts compressions, and Matt crumbles to his knees, both hands in his hair.

We all flinch.

"That's enough," Walker says, but the video doesn't stop playing, and not one of us seems to be able to stop watching.

Walker's hair falls over his eyes as he leans over my body, using all his weight to pump my chest. And then Matt yells something and charges him. They both fall to the deck of the boat, roll, and then in one swift movement, Walker's fist cocks back and swings forward at Matt, landing square on his cheek.

I glance at Matt, at the remains of the bruise there in that spot.

On the screen, Walker gets back up and scrambles over to me, puts an ear to my chest, then blows two breaths of air into my mouth. He goes back to the compressions while Matt lies crumpled on the boat deck.

The frame freezes, and silence hangs over us all for a moment.

Dana's not smiling anymore, and her voice is serious when she speaks. "Matt . . . Walker . . . do you want to tell us what happened between you two in that moment? I mean why, in the middle of a life-and-death situation, did you end up in a scuffle?"

Matt's jaw tightens, and he stares down and ahead of him, at some invisible spot the rest of us can't see. "I panicked," he says. He looks at me. "I heard her ribs cracking, and I panicked. I thought he was hurting her."

He leans forward and looks past me to Walker. "I wasn't thinking, going after you like that—I overreacted, and I don't blame you for . . ." He shakes his head.

Dana lets his sentence hang unfinished for a moment. I watch Walker for some sort of reaction, to try to get a read on him, but he sits statue-still in his chair, his expression unchanging.

"Do you think maybe you overreacted as well?" Dana asks him. She looks at the screen, which replays just the punch, this time in slow motion, before it freezes again.

Walker glances at Matt, then looks at Dana. "No," he says flatly. "But you do, I guess."

"That's not what I meant," Dana backpedals. "I mean, things like that can happen in the heat of the moment."

We're all quiet, and Walker just looks at her, unblinking.

"I had to," he says, with a note of finality.

Dana gives an almost imperceptible nod, and the video comes back on. For a few more seconds, Walker pumps on my chest, and Matt stays where he is on the deck of the boat, and then a voice behind the camera says, "That girl is gone. There's no way she's gonna live."

The screen goes black and Dana looks us all over carefully, without saying anything. I can feel the camera panning over our faces just as she is.

When she's stretched the moment for maximum drama, she turns to the camera and repeats the last thing said on the video in a low, serious voice, enunciating every syllable. "There's no way that girl is going to live."

Now she turns to me. "Most people who witnessed that probably would've said the same thing. But you did, and you're here, and you're okay. All thanks to him." She motions at Walker, who now avoids making eye contact with any of us.

"How did you know what to do?" she asks him.

I see his jaw tighten as he looks at the ground. "I've done it before," he says flatly.

"Really?" Dana seems genuinely surprised. "Where and when was that? Was it on the fishing boat? Out on the water?"

"No." Walker levels his eyes on her in a way that I think we all understand as "Stop asking me questions."

There's a brief moment when I think she's going to press the matter, but then she backs off and turns her attention to me.

"So, Olivia, let's talk about how it actually feels to *see* what happened to you. It's got to be completely surreal."

I want to tell her that showing the video without warning us feels like a cheap way to try to sensationalize her segment, that it wasn't necessary to make us sit here and watch it together, hoping for a reaction. But I don't. And this is a question I can actually answer. "It *is* surreal," I say. "It's like I'm watching someone else."

She nods with exaggerated empathy. "It's interesting that you say that. I was thinking of what that voice said at the end: 'That girl is gone.' Do you think there's any truth to that?"

"I don't understand what you mean."

"I just have to imagine that experiencing something as traumatic as this accident, and surviving, seems like it would have the potential to change your life in a very fundamental way. Is that girl gone? Have you changed?"

She pauses, giving me—or any of us—space to agree. All I can think of is that she doesn't know the half of it, and I'm so glad. I don't want to talk about any of this anymore with her.

None of us says anything, so she continues. "I mean, this seems to have brought the two of you closer," she says, gesturing at Matt and me and our hands clasped solidly on the couch between us. "And I can only imagine the gratitude you must feel for this person who was a stranger, who became your savior. There's a connection there now. One that will always be there. And this is the first time you've been face-to-face with him since the accident. Is there anything you'd like to say to him?"

There is—so much—and I thought I'd be able to say it all, but I can't. Not like this. Not in front of her and her cameras. And not in front of Matt either. I don't want to make him feel any worse than he already so clearly does by saying everything I want to say to Walker.

But this is my chance to thank him, and I at least owe him that. We don't know each other, and we don't share any history. I don't know if I'll see him again.

I know how uncomfortable this is going to make them both, but I let go of Matt's hand and I turn to Walker, who is as far away as he can possibly be on the other side of me. Every bit of his body language says *Don't touch*, so I don't reach out my hand to him like I want to. Instead, I try to catch his eyes, really catch them, and for a second, I do, and we're locked like that, looking at each other across the small space that feels like miles and miles.

"Thank you for what you did that night," I say.

There's a second where his eyes soften, and he gives the slightest nod, and I feel a flicker of connection because his guard comes down, just a little.

"For both of us," I add, wanting Matt to know I'm thinking of him too.

And just like that the wall goes back up. He nods again, then looks away.

Someone behind the camera makes a motion to Dana, and she focuses her attention on us. "Well. This really has been a miraculous story, and it's been SO good to have you all here. Let's hope that you continue to heal and recover, and maybe even come out of this with a whole new way of seeing the world. Thank you so much for coming." She looks at the camera. "And thank you for tuning in."

The guy behind the camera makes another motion, and the little light blinks off. "That was great, you guys!" Dana chirps. "Thank you so much!" She's smiling like we're all on the same team. Like she didn't just blindside us or ask uncomfortable questions, or any of that.

Walker stands and yanks the mic off his shirt. He tosses it in his empty seat and turns to Matt and me.

We stand too. Matt's face is serious, but he extends his hand across me, to Walker. "I know it's not enough, but thank you. Again. I don't know what would've happened if you didn't do what you did."

Matt puts his arm around my shoulder, and Walker glances at it, but seems careful to avoid my eyes. Then he looks right at Matt. "You would've lost her."

It's like a second punch. Beside me, I feel Matt flinch.

Walker looks at me. "You two take care."

I stand there, not knowing what to say to that. I'd wanted to thank him off camera, and hoped I'd have the right words to do it, but no words come after that.

He takes a step back. Shoves his hands into his jacket pockets. "I need to go."

He turns to leave, and Dana totters after him in her heels. "Thank you for coming, Walker! I'm so glad you changed your mind."

He doesn't acknowledge her, just keeps walking down the hall until he disappears.

I'd be lying if I said I didn't want to do the same thing. Especially when Matt turns to Dana, his jaw tight. "You didn't tell me he was gonna be here too."

"Oh," she says, innocently. "I didn't think he was, at first. Wouldn't even talk to me." She glances at me, the corner of her mouth turning up in a smile. "But something changed his mind."

Matt looks at me like I know what she's talking about. I raise my hands and give him a look that says *I have no idea*, because I really don't.

"Let's go," he says. "We're finished here." He takes my hand, but something is different about it this time. A tension I almost want to resist.

Dana puts a hand on my shoulder. "Thank you so much for coming in, Olivia. You truly are a miracle, and I can't wait for everyone to see this soon, probably in the next couple of days." She smiles at me, then glances at Matt, who just nods. We turn to leave.

He walks fast down the hallway, and I have to work to keep up, even with him pulling me along. When we reach the doors, he swings them open with more force than necessary, and Walker, who's leaning against the building, phone to his ear, looks up, watching us.

Matt is so intent on getting to his truck he doesn't see him, and I'm glad because now Walker is looking right at me with an expression that's hard to read. I feel that flicker of something there again, and think maybe Dana was right about what she said about there being a connection now, because of what happened.

I keep my eyes on his as we climb into the truck, as I close the door, and even as we back out of the parking space. I try to keep my eyes on him for as long as I can, this person who saved me. Who pumped blood into my heart, and breathed his own air back into my lungs, and who brought me back to life when it seemed I was long gone.

And when we round the corner and he disappears, I remember to breathe.

And I feel something besides pain, deep in my chest.

The drive home is silent. Heavy with things said and unsaid. I'm sure Matt is thinking of what Walker said to him. I am. It seemed unnecessarily harsh. And exactly what Matt didn't need to hear. I feel terrible for him, and I don't know what to say or how to make him feel better. I don't know what I would've done before—if I would've reached across the seat and rested a hand on his knee, or tried to talk about something else, or brought it up and talked it over. So I don't do anything.

I sit on my side of the cab and watch out the window as our little town goes by. Shops and restaurants that are a mix of familiar and new to me. People I know and don't know. I wonder how many of them will watch that interview and what they'll think. I wonder what my parents will say—how mad they'll be. And I wonder how I'll explain to them why I did it in the first place. I almost wish now that I hadn't. Walker was so hostile, Matt probably does too.

It's not until we pull into my driveway and park that he turns to me. "Liv. I'm so sorry."

The apology surprises me, since I feel like I'm the one who should be apologizing. "For what?" I ask.

He takes a deep breath, and then his words come out in one long string. "Where do I start—for asking you to do that interview, for not being able to get you out, for that night, for—"

"Stop," I say, reaching out to him.

He looks at me, startled.

"Please," I say. "Stop apologizing. We'll never get past this if you don't."

It's quiet a moment, and Matt looks down at his hands in his lap.

"I don't blame you, Matt—for any of it," I say. "So you need to stop blaming yourself, or we'll never move on."

I don't know where it comes from, but it feels true. Matt looks at me like he doesn't know what to say, but somehow I feel like I do. I turn to face him.

"So, what if we just take it one day at a time? Make plans to see each other again?"

Matt nods, but he still looks a little unsure. "Okay. But only if you want to. I don't want you to feel like we have to—"

"I want to," I say. And it's the truth.

He looks relieved. "Tomorrow, then?"

"I'm going to work with Sam tomorrow, but what about the day after? Maybe in the afternoon?"

"Yeah." He nods. "Yeah, that'd be good."

"Okay," I say.

"Okay," he repeats.

I reach for the door handle but don't pull it. We both sit there quiet, and I get the feeling it's because this is the moment we'd normally kiss good-bye, but he doesn't make any move to. So I try. I lean across the seat and kiss him lightly on the cheek.

"Bye," I whisper close to his ear before I pull away.

He looks at me with an expression I can't read. "Bye, Liv."

I get out and walk up my driveway, feeling like I somehow missed something, or did or said something wrong. I look back at him, no idea what it could be.

He gives a half smile and a wave back, then looks over his shoulder to back up. Part of me wants to wave him down and tell him to come back, wants to try to figure out what I'm missing so I can fix it. Another part feels like I should apologize for being distant, or different, or whatever I must seem to him. For not being the girlfriend he knew and had. She probably would've known what to say to him, but I don't. And so I don't wave him down, and I don't tell him to come back. I stand there on my porch trying to ignore a whole other part of me that feels relief when he puts his truck in drive and rolls slowly down the street.

NINETEEN

SAM PUTS HIS big, heavy hand on my seat and looks over his shoulder as we back up. "Okay, you gotta admit. That moment, when Darth Vader says he's Luke's father, is EVERYTHING. Am I right? You didn't see that comin', did ya?"

I yawn. "Sam. We've been over this. I *remember Star Wars.*"

"Yeah, but it has way more impact watching it the old way. We may have done it wrong the first time, but you got a second chance to see the greatest story ever told—in the right order. Tonight we can start on the new ones, but there's a lot we need to talk about first."

"Sam. I've seen them."

"*Years* ago," he scoffs. He reaches for the pack of gum in the center console, pops a piece in his mouth, and then offers me one.

I take it. "Thanks."

"How'd your top secret mission go yesterday? Can I know about it today? Now that it's over?"

"It was kind of a disaster. I don't want to talk about it, but I'm sure you'll find out about it soon enough."

"Intriguing," Sam says, "but I'm patient. I'll wait. Plus, this is a good song. Listen. You probably haven't heard it before." He turns up the music, and we don't say anything else the rest of the way. We don't have to, and I appreciate this about my brother. When we get down to the Embarcadero, he parks in the back of the Fuel Dock and shuts off the car. Then he turns to me, his face serious.

"Okay. The moment we step out of this car, and into the restaurant . . ." He makes his voice go as deep as it can. "Liv . . . I am your boss."

I roll my eyes.

"Seriously," he says. "You have to do what I tell you to do. And it's going to be GREAT." He pounds the steering wheel for emphasis.

"Perfect," I say. "Can't wait."

We get out of the car, and he unlocks the back door of the Fuel Dock. "Now that's the can-do attitude I'm talkin' about."

He walks in ahead of me, flipping on all the light switches, and I look around the place, which is about the size of a small trailer or a food truck.

"I don't know why, but I always thought this place was bigger inside."

Now Sam gives me a look. "You've seen the outside, right? Where'd you think we kept all that space?"

"Never mind," I say. "Show me what to do. *Boss.*"

Sam rolls up his sleeves. "Heh. Gladly."

He takes me through the morning-shift prep work—slicing tomatoes and onions, shredding lettuce, filling ice.

"When do I get to learn how to use the milk shake machine?" I ask, eyeing the old-fashioned, three-pronged machine.

He steps in front of it. "Not so fast. That's an advanced skill. You'll be starting with delivery to the docks, like you've done before. You get the food there fast, fresh, and with a smile." He pauses. "And you actually like that job because you get to walk around outside like a princess for a few hours and get paid for it while the rest of us slave away here, breathing in burger grease."

I think about the crazy line yesterday and delivery girl sounds good to me. "Fine," I say. "But if it's so much better to be out delivering, why don't you do it?"

"I'm not cute enough. Charlie likes to have you girls in your Fuel Dock T-shirts and shorts and deck shoes out there delivering. He thinks it's good advertising."

"That's kinda gross."

"It's not like you're in a bikini or anything. Besides, your FACE is kinda gross."

I laugh. "I forgot all about that joke until yesterday."

"You forgot about a lot of things, sister."

"No, I mean there were these kids—the Wagners? Who I took the food to yesterday?"

"Yeah, they've been coming here for the last few years. Customer number eighty-seven. Great family. Even better tippers."

"Well, I didn't remember them, or that. But the kids were using that joke on each other."

"As well they should. It's a good joke."

"They said I taught it to them."

"Well, you are their favorite delivery girl, and they order from us almost daily while they're here."

I'm quiet a moment, thinking about our conversation the other day. "They also said they're taking sailing lessons from Walker. Did you know he works down here?"

Sam goes to the big industrial fridge and grabs out a giant block of cheese. "Yeah. He's like Charlie's go-to guy for whatever needs to be done in the harbor. He works the fleet when the fish are running, teaches sailing when they're not. Sometimes even does maintenance."

"Do you ever talk to him?"

Sam unwraps the cheese and puts it on the slicer. He turns it on. "No more than anybody else," he says. "Guy keeps to himself." He glances at me, then focuses on catching the slices of cheese as they come out on the other side of the blade. "I think he likes it that way."

"Why?"

Sam shrugs. "I don't know. It was awesome, what he did for you—I'll give him that. And he's good with his sailing customers, but he doesn't seem interested in making friends with anyone here."

I nod. That seems accurate, based on the interview yesterday. "Do you think he doesn't like us? Because of that whole thing that happened with Mom reporting his parents?"

"I don't know. That'd be a long grudge to hold." Sam looks at me. "Why all the questions about Walker? Got a little crush on your hero?"

"No," I say quickly. "Geez, I was just curious what he's like, that's all."

"Uh-huh," Sam says.

We finish the last of the prep work just as the rest of the crew arrives and clocks in. Sam greets them all with a smile, introduces me as his delivery girl, and just like he said, we start to get busy around eleven. By eleven thirty, we're slammed with orders, so I put on my new sunglasses and head out to the docks with the first few deliveries. The docks and their slips are all clearly marked, and this time I have a cheat sheet with all the codes, which makes things easier.

I quickly discover that the people on their boats are generally happy because they're here on vacation, and even happier when they see their food arrive. It doesn't take me long to realize that a smile and a little small talk go a long way toward a good tip. I try to keep it short and light, and let them do most of the talking just in case I should know them, and it works. There are a few who I gather are returners from small things they mention, and I go along with it when they seem like they know me.

I drop off an order of burgers with a family who's visiting for the first time, and after telling them about a special beach where they can go hunting for sand dollars, I decide I'm not quite ready to go grab another order, so I take the long way back. I walk the boardwalk like part of the crowd, until I find a place to lean on the railing and look out over the bay. Most of the fishing and larger sailboats are already out for the day, but there are stand-up paddlers out for their morning lap, and farther out, Lasers and Sabots zigzag around each other as they learn how to tack and turn. They're too far away for me to see if Walker and the Wagner kids are in any of them, but I look for them anyway. Mostly, I look for him.

I think about Sam asking why I was asking about Walker,

and it's hard to put my finger on. It's not a crush, like he said. Walker was cold and guarded—definitely not interested in making friends. But I do want to see him again. I want to talk to him, because I don't like the way things were left after the interview. Because I didn't get to tell him how much it means to me, what he did. And because of the way it felt when he actually looked at me. Maybe I just want to believe what that reporter said about a connection after something like that. I feel guilty at the thought, but I know I felt something, and a tiny part of me thinks that he maybe he did too.

My phone buzzes with a text. Sam, asking if I got lost. I text him back that I'll be right there, but I do go out of my way one more time to pass by the Sailboat Rentals and Lessons hut. There's a guy behind the counter, but it's not Walker, so I just pass by without stopping.

When I get back, Sam gives me a look. "What'd you do, go home or something?"

"Sorry. I . . ."

"Here," he says, handing me three bags. "Daily Wagner kid order. They're not at their boat, though, they're over at the little swimming beach. And they don't have any cash. Jackson said to put it on his tab. Because we do that now, and they're starting one."

I look down at the large bag, which holds an awful lot of food for two kids.

"They wanted to buy lunch for their sailing teacher," he says. "I thought you might wanna bring this one." Before I can answer, he disappears back into the kitchen to grab the next orders that are ready.

I walk slowly. It's one thing to think about the possibility of seeing Walker again after yesterday, but it's another knowing that I will. I try to think of what I'll say. I can't exactly give a big, heartfelt speech about him saving my life in front of the kids. It might even be weird to say thank you again. But then, *not* acknowledging it seems strange too. I don't know how I'm going to face him, but now I have to.

I try to calm the butterflies as I walk, but by the time I reach the end of the sidewalk where the swimming beach is, they're swirling all the way up my chest and into my throat. I spot him right away. He's crouched behind a little sailboat, which is beached just outside the swimming area, holding a water gun. Jackson and Dylan creep toward him from the opposite side, communicating with a series of hand gestures, their own water guns at the ready. When Jackson gives the signal, they charge the boat, letting out wild warrior calls, and Walker jumps up to defend himself against the attack.

It takes all of thirty seconds for them to empty their guns at each other, and at the end of it, there is no winner—or maybe they're all winners. They're all soaked. They stand there laughing, claiming victory over each other, and it makes me laugh too, like I'm a part of it. I step over the low seawall, and Dylan sees me and comes running over.

"Liv, you just missed it!"

Walker's head snaps in my direction at the mention of my name, and the smile disappears from his face. He turns and reaches into the boat for a towel. I watch as he stands, back to me, and dries his shoulders quickly.

"We just crushed him in a water war, and now he has to buy us ice cream later, that was the bet."

"That's awesome . . ." I watch as Walker grabs a shirt and a hat out of the boat and puts them both on. "Lucky you," I say, taking a few steps down the beach.

Jackson comes up to meet me and takes the bags from my hand. "Oh, good, we're starving! Walker! I got us lunch!" he calls. He looks at me. "Your brother let me start a tab, so I ordered extra. You should stay." He reaches into one of the bags and comes back up with a handful of French fries that he stuffs into his mouth. "He even said you could."

"Who?" I ask, glancing at Walker.

"Your brother."

I look at him. "You asked him if I could have lunch with you?"

"Yeah," he says, with no other explanation. "C'mon," he says, motioning with his free hand.

For a second I wonder who this kid thinks he is, but

when he shoves another handful of French fries into his mouth, I realize he's pretty much Sam. The mini-version.

Dylan grabs my hand in both of hers. "Yes! Stay! Pleeaassseee!"

I glance at Walker again, and when our eyes meet, he starts to pack abandoned squirt guns into the boat.

"I'm not sure I . . ."

I don't get to finish answering because Dylan pulls me down the beach after her brother, where they already have their towels spread out as a makeshift picnic blanket. I watch Walker out of the corner of my eye as I sit. He busies himself with something in the little sailboat without any indication that he's going to join us.

Jackson pulls a cheeseburger and fries out of the bag and stands. "Dude, I got you lunch. Come eat."

Walker looks at him. "Thanks, buddy," he answers. Then he looks at me. "But I'm gonna need to take it to go. I need to get outta here—get the boat back."

The butterflies in my stomach fall like leaves to the ground. He's going because of me. I can feel it.

"Aw, I thought you were gonna eat it here on the beach with us." Dylan pouts.

"Next time," Walker answers, and he gives her a tight smile. "Promise. You guys have fun with Liv, here."

He turns and takes a few steps toward the boat, but then stops. His shoulders rise as he takes a deep breath, then he reaches into his pocket and pulls something out. Turns and looks at me, not the kids.

And then he comes back to where I'm standing. The butterflies take to the sky again.

We look at each other without saying anything for a moment, and his eyes soften like they did for just a split second during the interview, and it's the first time I've really gotten to look at him. His red baseball cap is turned backward, and his dark hair escapes from beneath it, curling up around the edges. I can feel myself looking too long at the way the stubble on his jawline comes up to meet it, but I can't help it.

He holds something out between us. "I found this on the boat. It's broken—I think it came off when . . ." He glances at the kids, whose eyes I can feel as well, then brings his eyes back to mine. "I was gonna give it to you yesterday, but that was . . ." He shakes his head.

"Kind of a mess," I say. And then I look down.

In his hand is a thin chain, broken, like he said. And next to it, the medallion that I recognize immediately but hadn't even realized was missing until just now.

"Wow," I say. "Thank you." I reach out and take both from his hand, hold the medal up in the sunlight. It makes me smile to see it. I look at Walker. "My friend brought this back to me from a trip she took to Italy when we were in seventh grade. She didn't know what it was when she bought it, and it was so funny when we looked it up because it turned out to be a Saint Anthony, who's the—"

"Patron saint of lost things," Walker finishes for me. "Guess it actually works."

I nod slowly. "I . . ." My head is swimming. "I was wearing this?" It surprises me, with the whole me-and-Jules-not-being-friends-anymore thing.

Walker looks at me strangely. "Yeah. Anyway. I need to get back." He turns and walks back to the boat before I can say anything else.

Dylan waves. "Bye, Walker!"

"See you tomorrow!" Jackson adds.

He gives the kids a wave, then pushes the little sailboat into the water and jumps in. And then, like it's nothing, he angles the boat away from the shore where I stand, without so much as a glance back. I watch as the wind catches and fills the small sail of the Laser, and I would keep watching until I can't see him anymore, but Dylan comes over and tugs on my hand again.

I look down at her and she smiles up at me.

"You lied. You guys are *totally* friends."

TWENTY

WHEN I GET back to the Fuel Dock, things have slowed down and Sam and a couple of guys are cleaning up the aftermath of the lunch rush.

"Wow, nice of you to come back," he says, as he wipes the counter. "I was starting to think you decided to take the rest of the day off."

"What? No, Jackson said you said I could have lunch with them, so I did."

Sam stops what he's doing. "Seriously?"

"Yeah. Seriously."

Sam laughs, and then shakes his head. "That kid. He's funny."

"You didn't tell him I could have lunch with them?"

"Why would I do that? You're on the clock."

I shrug. "I don't know, to be nice to your sister."

"Ha. No." He laughs again, harder this time, so that I have to wait for him to catch his breath. "What I *told* him was that I'd throw in an extra burger in case he had a cute girl he wanted to offer lunch to." He looks at me. "I guess you were it, though he could probably do better."

"Stop."

"What? It's true. You're way too old for him. But that was kinda smooth for a twelve-year-old, though." He looks over his shoulder. "Anyway, you can go home now. We're slowing down, and these guys need the hours, so they wanna stay. You feelin' okay? I'm not off for another hour, but I can walk if you wanna take my car home."

"I don't know how to drive."

"Balls. I forgot. We gotta fix that."

"I can walk. If you're sure it's all right for me to go."

He doesn't hesitate. "Yep, you're good. Get outta here, sport."

I laugh. "Okay. I'm gonna go."

Sam nods. "Good job today. See you at home."

"All right, champ."

I stop at his car to grab my purse and check my phone. There are multiple texts from both Paige and Matt, but I don't feel like answering them right now. I don't want to go home either, not yet. I don't know what I want. I feel aimless. Lost.

I pull the Saint Anthony from my pocket and run my thumb over the tiny medallion. I remember when Jules got home from her trip, she'd been so excited to give it to me. At first it didn't make sense, because she was never particularly religious, and neither was I. But then she told me how she'd wanted to buy something from a cute Italian boy who was selling them on the beach, and so that was my souvenir. That, and the story of how they'd gone for a walk after that, and he'd kissed her on the sand at sunset. And then it made perfect sense. Because I'd yet to have my first kiss, and was forever living vicariously through her.

When I'd asked her what the necklace meant, she didn't know, but said she'd seen a lot of surfers wearing them. When we'd looked it up, it turned out she'd bought the wrong saint. Surfers wore Saint Christopher medals. *This* was Saint Anthony of Padua, the patron saint of lost things, just like Walker had said. At first she'd been disappointed, because she'd been thinking it'd be cool to get me an Italian surfer necklace, but I'd told her I loved it anyway, and that I would always wear it in case I needed to find something I lost. And I guess I had.

Out of nowhere, a wave of sadness hits me, and I feel like I might cry at the irony of holding this thing in my hand. *So* much is lost to me, and I'm beginning to think it's actually gone for good. But Jules shouldn't be. I take a deep breath and tuck the Saint Anthony into my pocket, and in my mind I say the little prayer we found when we looked it up: *Anthony, Anthony, please come around. Something's lost that must be found.*

And then I make my way down Ruby Street, to In Focus, hoping to start there.

When I reach the shop, I can see Jules through the window, sitting behind the counter, reading a book. I take a deep breath and then push through the door.

She looks up, and her eyes widen in surprise for a moment, then she puts a slip of paper in her book and closes it. "Hi," she says, standing.

"Hi," I answer back.

It's quiet, except for the low sound of the machine printing photos behind Jules. She tilts her head. "You have some more film to drop off?"

I shake my head. "No, I . . ." I don't know where to start with this. "I just wanted to talk to you about something."

"Okaay . . ."

"It's—this is really strange for me, but it's also important, so I'm just gonna say it."

Her brows furrow. "Okay. What?"

"I lost my memory in the accident," I blurt. "Not all of it, but four or five years, and when I woke up and Paige was there, and you weren't, she said we weren't friends anymore, and I didn't believe her, but then the other night when I came in with Matt, it felt like we were strangers, so I knew it was true, and I don't understand, Jules—why aren't we friends anymore?" I take a breath, fight the tears I can feel rising behind my eyes. "What happened? With us?"

Jules doesn't say anything for a moment, just blinks in shock, or confusion, or both. The silence stretches out, and with every second, I'm sure it must've been something terrible. That I must've done something terrible.

Then slowly, she comes out from behind the counter to me, so we're standing face-to-face. "God, Liv," she says, and she puts her arms around me in a silent hug. "It doesn't matter, not with this happening to you. That was a long time ago."

I cry into her shoulder. "What? What was a long time ago?"

She pulls me back by my shoulders. "Nothing. Don't even worry about it. Are you okay? How are you doing *life* right now like this?"

I laugh and wipe at my eyes. "I don't know. I'm just lost . . . all the time—not literally—I still know my way around town, I just . . . don't really know my way around my life." It's a relief to say it out loud to someone who's not so closely tied up in it. I catch my breath. "So maybe you could just tell me the part about what happened to us," I say.

"Please? I just . . . I feel like I need to know."

Jules runs her eyes over my face like she's checking to be sure I'm okay. Then she shrugs. "It wasn't anything big or dramatic," she says, "so it's hard to even know how it started, but I remember feeling like we were growing apart." She pauses. "I hate to say it, because I don't want to blame Matt—he's a great guy—but you two got together and started hanging out with Paige and her boyfriend at the time, and I just kinda became the fifth wheel."

"I'm sorry," I say softly.

Jules waves a dismissive hand. "You don't need to be sorry." She smiles. "Not now, at least. My feelings were hurt at first, but then I started hanging out with other people too. That's what happens in high school. Groups break up, friends drift. People change. It's just how it goes sometimes. We didn't hate each other or anything, we just didn't really know each other anymore."

I sit there quiet, relieved that I didn't do anything terrible to her, but still sad at the thought of us just drifting apart like that. My phone buzzes in my pocket.

I check it. My mom.

Everything okay? Sam just got home and said you left work before him. Where are you?

"Sorry," I say to Jules. "I need to answer my mom real quick or she'll get worried."

"No problem," she says.

Stopped by In Focus. Heading home soon.

My mom texts me back a thumbs-up.

"Anyway," I say, looking at Jules again. "You're here for the next few weeks?"

She nods. "Yep. And this place doesn't see a whole lot of action, so feel free to stop by anytime." She squeezes my hand. "There's nothing that says we can't know each other now, right?"

"Right," I say. "I definitely will." And I know it's true. This feels right, her being a part of my life. Like a tiny bit of that big emptiness is gone.

I walk home feeling like I just found another little piece of myself that fits. It makes me want to tell Paige about it—and everything else that's happened in the last couple of days. She doesn't know about the interview, or work, or anything. I've been kind of a loner since I got home, and Paige has been trying so hard, and after talking to Jules, I want to make sure *we* don't drift too, so I decide to stop by her house on my way home.

There's so much I want to talk to her about. I go over it all in my head as I walk, order it into priorities: what just happened with Jules, how to fix things with Matt after that interview, my camera, the pictures, the things scrawled all over my wall, all of it. The walking and the cataloguing are calming, like I'm moving forward and have a plan, instead of being lost and grasping at things I can't remember.

Before I know it, I round the corner to her street, and I feel something I haven't since I've woken up. Hopeful for what's ahead.

Then I stop short.

At first I'm confused. I look around to make sure that I didn't get lost, that I still know the way to the house Paige has lived in ever since I can remember. I do a complete turn, check the street names, and verify that I'm definitely in the right place. It's just that there's something else that seems to be in the wrong place. And that thing is Matt's truck, parked in Paige's driveway.

I stand there frozen for a moment, trying to make sense of it, reminding myself that we're all friends. He probably went to her to talk too. Maybe even to ask her the same questions about how to handle everything that's happened to us. I turn off the sidewalk up to her walk. But then her front door opens, and the two of them come out together.

I duck behind a shrub and watch as they come down the walk to his truck. Their faces are serious.

Matt stops, rests one hand on the hood. He shakes his head, then looks at Paige. "I don't know. I'm trying, and I can tell she is too, but it's like she doesn't know me."

I bite my lip, because I can feel my eyes start to water at this.

Paige takes a step toward him, then rests her arm on the hood, mirroring him. "You have to give her time. I know she's different—I was over there the other day, and . . . it's hard. I think—" She pauses, shrugs. "I don't even think she knows *herself* right now."

Her words sting, and all the hope and reassurance I'd felt just moments before rush out of me. It's one thing to have thought it myself, but it's entirely different to hear Paige say it out loud. That I'm not myself. That I'm different than before. That I don't know who I am. But she's right, and until this moment I thought, or at least hoped, that maybe no one else realized that what I've been so afraid is true.

Paige brings a hand to Matt's shoulder. "We'll get her back, I promise. It's just gonna take a little time, and a few more gentle reminders of who she is, and what matters to her," she says confidently. "And hopefully it'll be even better than before."

Matt's quiet a moment, and I can almost feel the same question I asked my mom on the tip of his tongue: *What if it isn't?*

But he doesn't ask it. "I hope you're right," he says, mustering a smile I don't believe.

Paige smiles back, and I don't believe hers either. "I know I am, because I know Liv," she says. "Come on. Let's go get something to eat, and we can figure out what to do next."

He nods. "Yeah, okay."

They part, walk to each side of the truck, and get in. For a second I worry they might see me when they back up, and

I look around for somewhere to hide. But it doesn't matter. Matt's truck rolls right by me, with Paige saying something I can't hear, and him smiling at it, and it's like I'm not even there.

I watch, frozen, as my best friend and my boyfriend drive away together to figure out how to get me back, and what's next, whatever that means. I watch until they turn the corner and disappear, trying to sort out what I'm feeling. It's not anger or jealousy. Those would be easier, because there would be someone else to blame. But the only person to blame here is me. I feel like I've failed—at being Paige's friend and Matt's girlfriend. At being the girl they knew— or thought they knew.

The other thing I feel is a creeping sense of guilt. At what they don't know, and what I'm just beginning to know. That I'd been keeping secrets. Hiding things from the two people who were closest to me. Hiding myself, really.

TWENTY-ONE

WHEN I MAKE IT to my driveway, I get a sinking feeling in my stomach. My dad is supposed to be at work, but his car is here. At home. I take a deep breath, then go up the walk to our door. When I get there, I can see through the living room window that my parents are together. Waiting for me.

I can tell my dad must've called off work early, because he's still in his work boots and pants, and he's dressed down to the plain white T-shirt he always wears under his uniform. The TV is on. My mom is pacing.

The interview must have aired.

I stand on the step and take another deep breath, and then I open the door. Both of their heads swivel in my direction.

My mom stops pacing and crosses her arms over her chest. "Have a seat, please." Her voice has that barely-containing-her-anger shakiness to it.

I open my mouth to try to explain, but I don't get the chance.

"Go ahead and sit down, Liv," my dad says. His voice is calm. Good cop to my mom's bad cop.

Both of them look older and more tired than they should, even accounting for my time gap, and I feel guilty about doing the interview. And bad that they had to find out about it like this. Some tiny part of me was thinking that maybe they wouldn't even have to know about it, but I realize now that was foolish.

"What were you *thinking*, Olivia?" my mom practically spits as soon as I sit down. "An interview? With that woman?" Her voice rises with each question. "And God, the video." Her eyes start to water, and she goes quiet a moment. Then she takes a deep breath and lets it out in a sigh. "I wish you'd never seen that."

"I had to see it."

My mom shakes her head. "You shouldn't have. It's awful."

"Yeah, it is. But it happened to me, and to Matt, and I needed to see it."

My mom sits, massaging her temples. My dad puts a big hand on her shoulder and squeezes.

"Why the interview?" he asks. "Did that reporter come to the hospital? Call you? Pressure you into it somehow?"

"No. I . . ." I almost want to tell them that Matt asked me to, but I know that wasn't the only reason. I had my own reasons. "I called her," I say.

"Without asking us? Why would you do that?" my mom asks.

I look at my dad. "Because I knew you would've said no."

He nods. "Yeah. We would've. You don't need to be doing that right now. What you should be focusing on is healing and moving forward."

"That's what I'm trying to do." I bite the inside of my cheek to keep from crying. "But how am I supposed to do that if I don't even know everything that happened to me?"

"This isn't like you, Liv," my mom says. "Sneaking around, not telling us where you're going, not answering your phone calls. This isn't *you*."

It's that last part that puts me over the edge, especially after what I just overheard in Paige's driveway.

"Maybe that's because there IS no me anymore!" I surprise all of us with the force of my response. "Can't you see that? There's nothing there, it's just blank, and I was . . . I'm just trying to find out who I even am." I pause, look down at my hands. Rein myself in a little. "I thought it might help somehow, but it didn't. It just . . . made things worse. Matt hasn't called me since then, and Paige thinks I'm different, and I don't know what to do anymore."

I sit there wishing I could somehow stop the tears that have started streaming down my face without my permission.

It's silent for a long moment.

"Oh, honey," my mom says, crossing the space to the couch. She sits on the other side of me. "I'm so sorry. I didn't know you were struggling so much with this. You've seemed like you're doing okay . . ."

"That's because everyone wants me to be. Everyone wants me to just go back to normal, and I'm trying, I really am, but I don't even know what that is." I sniff. "And people keep trying to tell me what to do, and I know they're trying to help, but what if they don't even know who I was?"

I think of Paige saying she knows I'll go back to the way I was before because she knows *me*, but what if there's a part of me she doesn't know? What if I was one person with her, and someone else with Matt, and maybe even someone else with another person I don't remember? I still don't know what other secrets I'd been keeping, or why.

I look at my parents, who have both gone quiet. "What if *I* was the only one who really knew who I was before? Where does that leave me now that it's all gone?"

My dad takes a deep breath and gives my mom a look like he hopes she takes this one.

She does. "Liv, honey, figuring out who you are—whether you've had an accident or not—is what being a teenager is. It's what being a *person* is." She pauses, thinking, and then goes on. "Of course you were different when you were with Matt or Paige, as opposed to us. That's normal. We're all a little different around different people. I'm different at work than I am at home. Different with your aunt than I am with your dad. Even different with you than I am with Sam. But they're all small differences." She pauses again. "The point is, I'm the same person at my core. And so are you." She takes my hands in both of hers and lowers her chin until she catches my eyes. "You're not empty. The things that make up who you are? They're still there. They didn't go away just because you can't remember them. They're *in* you. So you just need to trust your gut. Really listen for what you think and feel. *That's* you."

My dad is nodding. "Yep. Like with the tacos that first night you were home."

My mom and I look at each other, and then at him for an explanation.

"What? When you reached for the meat and your mom reminded you that you were a vegetarian."

I laugh. "What?"

"Bruce. Tacos?" Now she laughs too.

My dad shrugs. "Yes, tacos. It's a perfect example of what you just told her." He looks at me now. "You gotta go with what seems right to you, not what you think you should be doing because it's what you've been told. You're allowed to change. We all are."

"Wow," my mom says. She smiles and reaches out for my dad. "Eloquently put."

My dad grins. "Sometimes the words just come to me."

Sitting there between my parents in that moment, I feel a little bit better. Like they just somehow gave me permission to be more okay with who I am right now. I wipe my tears away, trying to see myself from their perspective. One in which it's okay to be different from what people expect me to be. I don't feel like I'm there yet, but it doesn't seem like an unreasonable idea when I think about it that way.

"So here's the deal," my dad says. "From now on, maybe don't focus so much on trying to remember how you were. Stop thinking about that all the time. Just go with the now. Does that make sense?"

I nod.

"And talk to us," my mom adds. "Ask questions. Let us know what you're feeling. This is a tough situation, and one that you need to have support in. But we can't give that to you unless you let us know what you need, okay?"

I nod again. "Okay."

"Yep," my dad says, "we're always here if you want to taco 'bout it."

"Oh my God, Dad." I roll my eyes, but this gets me and my mom both laughing.

"Please don't ever say that again," my mom says.

Upstairs in my room, I sit down on the bed and check my phone—three more missed calls, two from Paige and one from Matt. I still feel a little unsettled about seeing them together earlier, but I tell myself that they both care about me, and they're both trying to figure things out the same way I am.

Still, I don't call or text them back. Not yet. I get up and take the three pictures from my bulletin board and examine the one of myself again, like maybe I'll see something different this time. I try to trust my gut like my mom said, and what I feel is that this picture of me is important. Because it was taken using my camera, and because I look so incredibly happy in it, and because whoever took it captured that moment. Captured me. More than any of the other pictures I've seen of myself. It makes me think if I find the person behind the camera, then maybe I can find myself—and Matt and Paige are my two best options.

I'm sitting there, staring at the photo, when my phone buzzes with a text from Paige.

Everything okay? Worried about you. Call me please???

I stare at it a moment, then hit the button to call her back.

She answers right away. "Hey—is everything okay? You've been MIA for the last couple of days, and Matt said you're not answering his calls or texts either, and I was just worried about you. What's going on?"

"I'm fine," I say, picturing them driving away together, and thinking I should probably ask her the same thing. But something in me decides to let it go. "Sorry," I say. "We did family movie night last night, and then I had to work today. I just haven't really had a chance to call."

"Gotcha. That makes sense. How was your first day? Did Sam take advantage and order you around all day?"

"Not too much. I was actually out delivering most of the time, so it wasn't bad."

"That's good!" she says brightly.

The line goes quiet, and I still have so much to tell her, but I ask her a question instead.

"Hey—this is kind of random, but did you ever take a picture of me with my camera?"

Paige laughs, and I hope this means the answer is yes. All this would be so much easier if her answer is yes. She would know what was going on with me if the answer is yes.

"I've taken lots of pictures of you," she says.

"I mean with my actual camera."

"The old one you used to lug around everywhere? Liv, what are you . . . ?"

"Never mind," I say, and I try to keep the disappointment out of my voice. "I was just going through some old pictures, and there was one I really liked that I thought you might've taken."

"I doubt it. You never let anyone else touch that camera." I think about it, and she's right. I didn't trust anyone with it. Especially not to take pictures of me. "Anyway," she says, "are you and Matt still gonna hang out tomorrow? He said you guys made plans the other day, but he hadn't heard back from you."

"Yeah, I . . . I need to call him back next."

"You want me to come over and help you get ready again?"

"No—I mean, that's okay. I'm good."

"Well, I'm here if you need me, even just for moral support."

"Thanks."

"And give me a call after. Let's hang out."

"I will."

"Good. Love you, Liv."

"Love you too."

I hang up and take a deep breath. Get ready to call Matt next. We haven't spoken since he dropped me off after the interview, so I'm not sure what to expect. He answers on the first ring too.

"Liv, hi."

"Hi."

"How are you?" he asks. "How'd your first day of work go?"

"Fine, it was good."

"Good."

There's a long pause on the line.

"So did you still wanna hang out tomorrow after you get off work?" he asks.

"Yeah, I do. I'm off at three, so maybe pick me up at three thirty?"

"Sure. That sounds good."

"Okay," I say.

"Okay," he repeats.

We both laugh.

"See you tomorrow, Liv."

"See you tomorrow."

I hear him laugh again as I hang up, and I hope this isn't the way the whole thing goes tomorrow. I think of what he said to Paige, about both of us trying. He still is. And if he's willing to try for us, then I think I am too, but I need to see him again to know for sure.

I get up to get in the shower, but remember my necklace

in my pocket. I don't want to lose it again, so take it out and set it next to the pictures. And then, for good measure, I repeat the little poem in my mind.

I sit there a moment, phone in my hand. And then I tap the Instagram button and scroll through my own feed for the umpteenth time, looking through all the photos of me and Matt for I don't know what. A shot that'll make me excited to see him tomorrow? A picture of us that'll evoke something familiar in me? I've already memorized the first frames that show up, so I keep scrolling, back, and back, looking for anything that might have that kind of effect. Anything that will convince me that we are still right for each other. That I actually should still be trying.

And then I land on something. A photo I hadn't paid any attention to before. Hadn't even seen—maybe because it's one of the only shots not filled with smiling faces. I click on it to get a better look.

This one is just of the sky and a crazy swirl of clouds, lit from beneath by the setting sun. It's beautiful, a breathtaking moment, and I wonder if this is one of the shots Chloe was talking about, where I was working on capturing light. I examine the fiery horizon, and the dusky ocean, and then something that's just barely in the frame catches my eye. It looks almost like it could be a mast, and there is a hand resting on it. I look down to see what I wrote about it, but there is no caption. It's the only one, out of them all, that has no caption.

But looking at it now, there's that feeling again, that this means something.

TWENTY-TWO

THE NEXT DAY, work goes by in a blur of deliveries that don't go very well. I make mistakes, get lost, take too long, because I'm not really there. I'm in my mind, still sorting through conversations and stories and pictures and details. I try not to feel frustrated, try to just go with the now, like my dad said, but today it feels like everything I need to know is right there below the surface, beneath some invisible, impenetrable barrier that's in place for me alone.

After work, I shower and change but don't have time to put on any makeup or do my hair like Paige did before Matt arrives to pick me up, and his surprise shows on his face when I answer the door.

"Hi," he says, with an awkward smile. "You ready to go,

or did you need more time?"

"I'm ready—unless I need to dress up. Do I need to dress up?"

He shakes his head. "No. You're perfect just like that."

We get into his truck, I remember how to work the seat belt, and all of it feels more familiar this time.

"So," I say, as we drive out of the neighborhood, "where are we headed?" I try to keep my tone light. This is the first of many questions I need to ask him.

He smiles. "You'll see. It's kind of a surprise."

"Okay."

We're both quiet as he pulls onto the highway that heads north, out of town, then he glances over at me. "So. How was work?"

"Busy. Crazy. How was yours?"

"It was good." He smiles. "Finally got this little guy who was terrified of the water to let go of the wall and swim halfway across the pool to me. He was pretty proud, so that was a win."

"Aw. He's gonna remember you for that."

I cringe even as the words come out of my mouth.

Matt glances over at me. "Maybe. I mean, I hope so."

He drives, and I look out the window, and it's so quiet I roll mine down, just to have something other than the silence between us because I can't think of anything to say. At least, nothing that I'm ready to say yet.

"So this place we're going," he says finally. "It's where I took you on our second date. You packed a picnic, and we just sat on the beach and ate and hung out, and I was thinking it would be nice to do that again." He looks at me. "Does that sound okay? I mean, we can do something else if you want."

"No," I say. "That sounds really nice. You should've told me, though—I would've packed us a picnic again."

"I took care of it," he says, and motions to the backseat of the truck.

Sitting there on the seat is a neatly folded blanket and picnic basket.

"You did that?"

"I had a little help," he says. He looks at me. "Paige."

"Ah. She's good with that sort of thing." I laugh a little. "She probably helped *me* out with it the first time."

"Maybe," he says.

We're both quiet, and the silence stretches so tight you could burst it with a pin. We both start to say something.

"I'm not really—"

"We don't have to—"

We stop. Laugh awkwardly. Matt looks at me. "Sorry. What were you gonna say?"

Now I wish I'd just let it be. He looks so nervous. But I don't know if I'm actually up for a picnic—or trying to re-create our second date. I clear my throat. "I just . . . I'm not very hungry, so I don't know if—"

"It's okay," he says quickly. "We don't have to go all the way up there. It was just an idea. Just a place to go."

I glance up the road and see a park near the beach. "Can we maybe just park over there? Take a walk or something?"

"Sure, yeah." He takes the next exit, pulls into the parking lot of the beach park, and shuts the truck off. Looks over at me like he's waiting for a cue to follow.

As soon as I reach for my door handle, he does the same. We get out, and he lets me lead, which I do, to a bench at the edge of the sand. I'm not quite sure what I want to ask him first, but I can feel myself working up the nerve to start. I think he must be able to feel it too, because when we sit, he swallows hard and then looks at me.

"Is everything okay with you? You seem . . ."

"I haven't really seemed like myself to you, have I?"

"That's not what I meant, I just . . ."

"I know." I look out at the ocean, and the whitecaps coming in with the wind. "I guess I'm not. But I'm okay. I think."

I honestly don't know, and trying to explain it isn't going to be easy. I take a deep breath, then force myself to look at him. "There are some things that have been . . . that I've been thinking about . . ." I look down at my hands. "There's just a lot that I don't understand, or that doesn't make sense to me right now."

Matt looks nervous when he nods. "Me too."

"This is gonna seem strange, but I need to ask you something," I say. I take the picture of me out of my purse and hand it to him. "Did you take this picture of me?" I ask. I try to ignore the feeling that I already know the answer.

He takes it and looks at it. Shakes his head. "Wow, no. I wish I did, though. It's really pretty." He hands it back to me. "You really don't know who took it?"

I shake my head. "No."

A wave rises in front of us, and we're both quiet as we watch it crash on the shore.

"I need to ask you something else, then."

"Okay," Matt says slowly. His voice matches the sudden seriousness of my own.

"Were we happy before the accident? You and me?" The words come out before I have a chance to choose them more carefully.

Matt looks about as ready to answer this as I felt to ask it.

"I . . . yeah, I mean we . . ." He fumbles. Bites his lip. Looks at me. "What do you mean?"

He looks a little wounded by the question, and I feel guilty for asking, but there's something else that I feel. Something that I trust more than my guilt. It makes me brave enough to push it.

"I mean the two of us, as a couple. Were we still happy?"

"I don't understand where this is coming from, Liv.

Why are you asking me this?"

"It's just . . . I was thinking about what you said last time, about how doing the interview would help with what people were saying."

He tenses, and I feel like I'm on the right track. I ease ahead, trying to trust what I feel.

"And then the other day, I was gonna go see Paige, but your truck was—you two were together."

Matt takes a deep breath and lets it out in a long, slow exhale. I expect him to reach for my hand and explain it away, or at least to look at me. But he does neither. He keeps his eyes on the water in front of us.

The knot in my stomach tightens, but I ask another question. "What was going on with us before the accident? What are you not telling me?"

Matt runs his hands through his hair, a gesture I now recognize as nervous. "I swear, nothing's happening with Paige, if that's what you think."

"Okay," I say slowly. "So what were you doing with her yesterday?"

"Just . . . talking. About what to do."

"About me?"

"Yeah," he says. And now he turns and looks at me. Runs his eyes over my face, and I see sadness in his. He looks down at his hands.

"What?" I ask, more nervous than ever now. I'm afraid

of what he's going to say. I'm afraid that the reason he looks so sad is going to be my fault because there really was someone else, and maybe that's why we were drifting, like I told Sam. But I can't handle not knowing. Not anymore. I need to know what I did. "Matt. What is it?"

He looks up at me again, and now his eyes are watery. He presses his lips together and swallows hard.

"We broke up the day before the accident."

"What? Why?" I ask, even though I'm sure now of the answer, and I'm ready to hate myself for it.

"I . . ." He takes in another deep breath and rubs his forehead. "I broke it off. With you."

"You did? *Why?*" My voice is just barely above a whisper. Matt can't even look at me.

"Because I . . . we . . ." He shakes his head. Shrugs. "We were just drifting. For a long time. I mean. We'd been together for so long, but it wasn't the same anymore. We weren't the same. And that day, for whatever reason, I just knew that was it. I told you I thought we should break up."

He looks at me now, his eyes wet.

"You cried. But you didn't argue. Because you knew it too." He rubs his lips together. "So I guess it was both of us, but . . ." He shakes his head again. "I don't know if it would've happened if I hadn't said it, you know? Because it didn't feel good. I wasn't happy after. Or relieved. I was just empty and sad and lonely."

He looks at me now.

"That's why I went out to that party on the island the next night. Just to try and shake it off. But then when I started drinking, all I could think of was you, and so I called you, and you said you'd come get me."

He pauses again, shakes his head. "I shouldn't have let you. If I didn't call you that night, we wouldn't have been on that bridge. And this wouldn't have happened to you. You have no idea how many times I've wished I could take that back, Liv. All of it."

He looks at me now, gives me the space to say something. Anything. But I can't. And so he keeps going.

"I just wanted to see you again. I knew I'd made this huge mistake, and I wanted to take it back, and I thought if I could just see you again, we could act like it didn't happen, and go back to how we were before."

I force myself to keep my eyes on his, but I feel far away, like I'm watching us from a distance. Like this isn't really happening.

"You came all the way out there to pick me up, and I tried to take it back. I told you that, and I tried to kiss you—because I couldn't remember the last time we'd even kissed. But you just pushed me away, you were so mad."

He pauses again, and I try to picture it.

"You put me in your car anyway. And then . . . you know the rest."

"No," I say. "I don't. I don't know any of this."

He looks down and takes another deep breath. "You told me we really were done. And that you'd known it too."

We both stare out at the water. He shakes his head, helpless.

"And then the accident happened, and I couldn't get you out—" He puts his head in his hands. "You would've died if Walker hadn't shown up—because of me. You would've died. And when he pulled you out of that water, I saw how much I would've lost, and how much I loved you." He pauses. Corrects himself. "How much I love you."

We're both quiet. Another wave crashes on the beach in front of us, and the water rushes back down the sand to the ocean. I wish I could go with it.

"I'm sorry, Liv. I know should've told you. I just . . ." He looks at me. "I just thought maybe this was our second chance, that this could be—"

"Did Paige know?" My voice sounds small. "That we broke up?"

Matt looks down at his hands, and I know the answer before he says it. "Yeah," he says quietly. "I asked her if she'd help me try again with you—to make it right—because I'd screwed it up so bad."

I laugh, and it startles both of us. "To make it *right*? How is anything about this right?"

"I made a mistake, Liv. I realized that at the party, and

then out there on that boat, and when you were in the hospital, and then again when you woke up. We belong together, and—"

"Do we?" I wipe at my eyes. "Or do you just feel guilty?"

Matt goes silent.

"Because that's worse. That's worse than growing apart, or falling out of love, or even lying. Being with someone because you feel guilty is worse." As I say the words, I realize they're not just for him. They're for me too. I need to hear them for myself.

"That's not it," Matt says. "That's not how it is." But there's no conviction in his voice. Nothing behind those words. He sounds the same way I would if I tried to say what he's saying.

"Yes," I say. "That is it."

Matt shakes his head. "What do we do if it is?"

It's quiet for a long moment.

"We let each other go," I say finally. "Again."

I don't expect to, but I start crying when I say it. Because it's not just letting each other go, it's letting something bigger go. It's the idea of us, and of who I was with him, and in all those pictures of us together.

I turn and look at Matt, who began as a stranger to me. Who loved me once. And who I loved back. And in that moment, I regret not ever knowing the feeling of that. I regret not having those memories—the days and nights we spent together, the moments only the two of us knew about—all our firsts. And now, our lasts.

I don't want it to be over without adding my own. One last moment of us, together.

And so, sitting there on that bench, shivering as the wind comes up, I bring my lips to his, and I kiss him. I kiss him, just like I did that first time, except this kiss is different. There's no spark of excitement or connection. It's not a beginning, or a hope, or the promise of something new.

It's a good-bye.

TWENTY-THREE

"LIV? IS THAT YOU?"

My mom comes around the kitchen corner, drying her hands with a dish towel, looking surprised to see me. "Hi, sweetie." She glances at the driveway. "Is Matt gone already? Sam said the two of you were going out for a bit. I thought maybe he'd want to stay for the evening. We heated the pool up, and your dad's going to do some ribs, and it's been a while since we've had him over."

"He just dropped me off," I say, and I head for the stairs.

"Why don't you call him," she says with a smile. "I bet he'll come back if he knows Dad's grilling."

"Maybe another time." I try again for the stairs.

"You sure? It's could be fun to all relax together."

"Not today, okay?" My voice is flat and hard, and my mom's smile takes a tumble.

"Okay, no problem," she says, her tone changing, like she understands to stop pushing. "Another time, like you said."

I look at her now. "Actually, there won't be another time."

"What?" she asks, like she heard me wrong. "What do you mean?"

I'm about to say I broke up with him, but that's only partially true. "We broke up," I say instead.

"What?" She brings the hand still holding the dish towel to her chest. "Just now? Oh, honey, I'm so sorry."

That "Oh, honey," and the note of sympathy in her voice, does me in. It always has. A lump springs to my throat, and my eyes water, but I fight it. I don't want to cry right now, in front of her.

"What happened?" my mom asks. She steps toward me, arms open for a hug, and I fight the urge to take a step back. That'll just make it worse.

"I . . . I don't really want to talk about it right now," I say, and I let her hug me for a moment. "I kind of just want to go be by myself for a while." Now I step back. "Is that okay?"

"Of course, sweetheart. I understand."

"Thanks."

"You need anything?"

I shake my head.

"I've got some good chocolate stashed in the pantry. Keep it just for emergencies like this."

I smile for her benefit, because she's trying so hard. "Maybe later."

"All right," she says, but she doesn't make a move to go anywhere.

My phone buzzes in my pocket, so I do. I don't have to look to know it's Paige. I reject the call on my way up the stairs. It rings again, and I reject it again and wait. She doesn't try a third time. I'm glad. I hope she doesn't come over. Of course my mom would let her in. Of course she'd expect that I'd want to see Paige and talk to her about Matt. I bet I did the first time.

But I don't even know if I could look at Paige right now. Especially when I think of her telling me how much I loved Matt, and how perfect we were together. I don't know what she thought she was doing, or how she thought that choosing what he asked her to tell me over telling me the truth was a good thing. It's the same with Sam keeping what he knew from me. And maybe, in more ways I don't even know about yet, my parents have kept things from me too. I'm sure they all justify it to themselves somehow—whether it's to make things easier on me or to somehow protect me. But it's the worst feeling in the world to think that everyone who knows you has what they think is a good enough reason to lie to you.

I go into my room and shut the door behind me. Stand there a moment, not knowing what to do. What I do know, what I'm almost certain of, is that Paige is probably on her way over here right now to try to apologize, or explain, and I can't do this with her right now. I can't.

I start to leave, to go I don't know where, but then I see my camera case sitting on my desk, a new box of film on top of it, with a Post-it and a note scrawled in my mom's writing:

> *Happy to see you found your way back to something*
> *you love. Here's to making new memories and seeing*
> *where they lead you!*

It stops me, right where I am, and cuts through my anger to something more fragile. The hope, maybe, that I can move on from this. I read the note over again, knowing that she means well, but it puts a lump in my throat just the same because even if I know this one thing about myself—that I like to take pictures—what good is it if it's the only thing? And what good are pictures, even, if I can't remember the story behind them?

They're useless.

Pictures aren't going to bring my memories back. They're not going to give me my life back either. Those things are gone, and the relationships that were part of them are gone too. They stayed the same, and I changed, and now I don't fit anymore. I look around my room that still doesn't feel like it belongs to me, with its decorations I don't remember choosing, and photos I never smiled for, of events I've never attended. Awards I've never won. The old me did all those things. And maybe I need to let them go.

I look up at the chalkboard wall in front of me, full to the edges with jokes and memories that I am no longer a part of. I never had Paige finish going through them with me, but that doesn't matter now. I open the drawer and find a chalkboard eraser that looks like it's never been used, and then I start in one corner. Memories that belong to me but don't disappear in seconds beneath the wide arc of the eraser. There are years' worth of moments that made up my life, and who I was—not just to my friends and family, but to myself. I wipe them away, one by one, and by the time I'm finished, the wall is a swirly mess of multicolored chalk dust. My desk is covered in it, and so am I, but when I stand back and look at it, what I feel is a small measure of relief at the destruction. Like I can almost breathe again.

I tuck the picture of me into my back pocket and go downstairs, and tell my mom I need to get some air so I'm going for a walk. She doesn't say anything about the chalk dust all over me. She just nods like she understands.

I don't know where I'm going when I step out the door, but I head for the beach, and when I hit the sand I stop for a moment. Take one breath, and then another. The sun hasn't set yet, but it's tucked away behind the expanse of gray clouds that have gathered on the horizon. The air is already cooling, and it makes me wish I'd brought a sweater, but it's too late now. I can't go back. Just like with everything else in my life. All I can do at this point is keep going forward. So I do. All the way down the beach.

I pass the harbor where boats are coming in, making their way home for the evening, and the Embarcadero, where tourists are starting to do the same. I don't even feel like I belong here anymore, so I keep walking, head down against the rising wind, putting one foot in front of the other. Moving forward. It's not until my feet hit the sidewalk of the Carson Bridge that I slow my steps and realize that I haven't moved forward at all. I've just gone backward, back to the place where this all started. Back to the beginning of this, and the end of me.

I stop for a moment to catch my breath. And then I keep going.

The sidewalk rises in front of me with the arc of the bridge, and my steps slow down—not because of the incline, but because of the increasing tightness in my chest, and the knowledge that I'm nearing the exact place where my car went over the bridge. I can see the tire marks on the road. They go across one lane and into the other, and then they disappear at a new section of cement. I check for cars, and when there are none, I follow the tire marks across the lane to the other side.

And then I'm here. In the place where everything changed. Where, moments before the video started rolling, a trucker lost control and crashed into my car, sending Matt and me careening into the water below. I stop. Close my eyes. And though I know it's not a memory, I see it happening. I see the truck's headlights in the rearview, and the moment we both felt fear—that fraction of a second that was the dividing line between before and after.

And then I see the impact. The explosion of glass, and the twist of metal before the free fall. The second impact, when we hit the water. The muffled silence that followed. The cold water pouring into the car as we sank. Filling my lungs and slowing my heart.

And then nothing.

That's what happened here.

I died.

And yet here I am.

I rest my elbows on the rough cement of the railing and lean over it. Look down into the water below. It's calm. Slick and dark on the surface, giving nothing away. No indication of what happened here. It's been forgotten already. The memory of it washed away with the ebb and flow of the tides, and carried out to the open ocean to be let go.

I put my head down on my arms, and I cry, finally. I cry

for this thing that happened to me, and everything I've lost, and the way I've tried and failed to find it. I cry for the past that's disappeared, and the present that doesn't fit right, and the future I can't see. But mostly I cry for the utter loneliness I feel in this moment.

The tears trickle down my cheeks and fall, and I let them. I let them all go until I have no more. And then I'm still, staring out at the water and the sky as dusk deepens the sky, and the lights in the harbor begin to blink on. I know I should go home, but I don't know how to get there from this place no one else inhabits or can even reach.

"Hey," a voice says, interrupting my thoughts. "Don't jump, okay? I got lucky the first time. I don't think we should count on it happening again."

I wipe at my eyes as I turn to see Walker standing there on the bridge. I look around. "What are you doing here?"

"Walking," he says simply. "What are *you* doing here?"

"Same." I don't offer an explanation even though I'm standing on the bridge where I almost died, crying.

He takes a step closer. "Do you . . . wanna walk somewhere else? You're making me kind of nervous up here like this."

I nod. "Okay."

So we walk.

We don't say anything at first. It's quiet, and I am keenly

aware of our steps, and my breathing, and the proximity of his shoulder to mine as we walk. He seems to be giving me space. The opportunity to talk or not, so I try to give him the same. It should feel strange, but it doesn't, being together like this.

We get to the end of the bridge and turn, head back toward the harbor, and once we're under the lights of the Embarcadero, he looks at me.

"So, trouble in paradise or existential crisis?"

"Both," I say without hesitating.

He nods. "Wanna talk about it?"

"No." I shiver.

"You cold?"

"A little."

He stops. Takes off his fleece-lined denim jacket and offers it to me. "Here."

I hesitate for a moment, not really sure why he's being so nice, or what it is we're doing, but then I take it and wrap it around my shoulders, and this doesn't feel strange either. There's a trace of warmth in the fabric, a clean, fresh smell that's almost familiar.

"Thank you," I say.

He just nods, and we keep walking, and when I'm sure he's not looking, I tuck my nose down into the collar, and breathe in, trying to place the scent. Nothing comes to me.

"You want me to walk you home?" Walker asks.

I shake my head. "No. I'm not ready to go home yet." And then a thought occurs to me. "There's something here I want to see."

"Okay," Walker says, holding his hand out in front of us. "Lead the way."

A little wave of hope rolls through me as I turn down the main dock, and head toward E Dock. When we reach it, Walker stands back, and I punch in the code that I remembered that first day when I came looking for *Second Chance*. I can't help but smile when the gate opens for me just as it did before.

Walker gives me a funny look, like he's humoring me or something.

"Just wait," I say.

We go through the gate, and he closes it gently behind us.

"You might know it already, since you live down here, but when I was younger, there was this old sailboat I used to love, called *Second Chance*." I glance at him as we walk, and he looks even more perplexed. "I'm sorry," I say. "It'll just take a second. I just want to see if it's still here."

"What do you mean if it's still here?" Walker asks as I pull him along, feeling almost desperate now to get there.

"I mean if it's . . ."

I stop just short of the last slip on the dock and blink, trying to reconcile the boat that's floating in front of me with the one in my memory. In the lights from the dock, I can see the name *Second Chance*, in the same spot where it always was. But the letters aren't faded to gray anymore. They're sharp, and black, and they stand out against the bright white paint of the hull. The wood of the cabin is varnished a warm, honey gold that shines even in the dim light, and the mainsail is wrapped neatly in a bright red cover.

I gasp. "Oh my God."

"What?" Walker asks, concerned.

I turn to him. "Do you know whose boat this is? Who fixed it?"

Walker looks at me with this strange look on his face. "You're joking, right?"

"No, I—" I look from him to the boat, and back again, confused.

"Are you really asking me?" he says, his eyes running over my face, searching for something. His voice softens. "About the boat? You really don't know, Liv?"

"Know what?"

Walker opens his mouth and starts to say something but stops. I see the muscles of his jaw tighten.

"Know what?" I repeat a little louder. Now I'm getting

worried. Something isn't right, I can tell from the look on his face.

Walker looks at the boat for a long moment before he brings his eyes back to me.

"*We* did this, Liv. We fixed it together."

TWENTY-FOUR

MY STOMACH DROPS. I look at Walker, the boat, the sky. Anything to try to make sense of what he just said.

"What?" I barely get the word out.

"We fixed it together."

I look at him, at the way his expression has turned into a mix of confusion and hurt, just like Matt's that day in the hospital, and I know he's telling me the truth.

"When?" I ask.

"For the last few months. Do you not . . ."

He doesn't finish the question, but I know what he's asking.

I shake my head, and I don't know if it's the dock swaying, or what he's telling me, but I feel dizzy all of a sudden.

Walker puts a hand on my shoulder to steady me. "You okay?"

I feel like I'm going to cry again any second. "No."

"Here," he says, "sit down."

He puts an arm around my shoulders and guides me over to the boat, helps me step onto it from the dock, and we sit together on the wooden bench. I close my eyes for a moment to try to steady myself while a storm of frantic questions crashes around in my mind.

I feel Walker get up, and I open my eyes. He disappears into the cabin and then is right back with a bottle of water that he opens and hands to me. "Here. Take a sip." I do, and as he watches me, I can see the worry on his face. "What's going on, Liv?"

I take a deep breath and another sip of water. "What were we?" I ask. "Because I don't . . ." I know I have to tell him that I don't remember, but the idea of saying it to him makes me feel lost and helpless all over again. And so sad, because this has happened before, with Matt, and I know how it goes.

My voice shakes when I speak. "Because I don't remember." I pause, trying to calm the tremor in my voice and read Walker's reaction at the same time. Trying to see if what I suspect is true. "Since the accident," I say, "I don't remember a lot of things."

"Like . . . ?" He puts his hands out, and I can tell he

doesn't even know how to finish the question.

"Like anything, from the last few years." I look down at my own hands in my lap. "The last thing I remember from before the accident is the summer before I started high school."

I look at Walker. He's quiet, and I can feel something shift between us. He leans back against the bench and looks out over the water.

"Wow" is all he says.

"I'm sorry," I say. "That's why I didn't know, just now . . ." I look around at the boat. "*We* did this?"

He laughs, but there's no joy in it. "Yeah."

"How did that even . . . ?" Now I don't know how to finish the question. "Is this your boat?"

He smiles, but it's brief and a little sad. "No. It's Charlie's. He made me a deal—work as rent, so I was fixing it up."

He pauses. Takes a deep breath and then looks at me. "You came down with your camera one day and told me that same thing you did a few minutes ago, about how you'd always loved this boat."

I try to picture it—him, working on the boat, and me, walking up with my camera.

"You asked if you could take a picture of it, and I said yes, so you did. Lots. And then you stuck around. Started asking a bunch of questions about what I was doing, until I finally just handed you a sanding block, hoping that if you were working you might not talk so much."

I laugh at this, because it's not hard for me to imagine. I have an endless list of questions I want to ask him right now.

"It didn't work," he says, and a smile tugs at the corners of his mouth. "You kept taking pictures and asking questions, and then you asked if you could come back the next day and help work on it."

"And you said yes?"

He nods.

"And I did?"

"Most days, yeah."

I look around at the boat, then at him as he does the same, and when our eyes meet, I feel a little flutter of something in my chest. "And we . . . worked together?"

He laughs in a way that sends a wave of nervousness all through me. "Kind of. I worked. You mostly took pictures."

"Of what?"

"The boat, the water, the sunset. Whatever caught your eye."

Pay attention to your attention.

"You?" I ask.

The question sends a wave of heat to my face.

Walker looks at me for a long moment, his eyes unreadable. "Sometimes."

My mouth goes dry, and my heart pounds in my chest,

and for just a second I picture us, here together on this boat.
"So we . . . ?"

I don't need to finish for him to know what I'm asking.
Walker's eyes run over my face, and he leans closer. Close
enough so that I can see the little flecks of gold in his eyes.
"No," he says. "You had your boyfriend, and your life, and
everything else."

He pauses, and I can almost see that wall of his come
back up.

"This was . . ." He shrugs. "Just a place you came to get
away from it sometimes."

He doesn't look at me when he says it, and I know it's not
true. I know that, just like everyone else, he's not telling me
everything. So I risk trusting myself. I reach into my back
pocket for the picture of me, and I unfold it between us.

"You took this picture, didn't you?"

He looks at it but doesn't say anything, and that's how
I know I'm right. "I was really happy when you took it,
wasn't I?"

His eyes linger on the image of me for a moment longer,
and then he looks at me. "Yeah. We both were."

"Why?"

"Because we'd finished the boat, and we took it out for
a sail."

"Do I know how to sail?" I ask. "Did you teach me?"

Walker laughs. "I tried."

"And we went to Vista Island together."

Hope rushes into his face. "Wait, you—"

"No," I say, shaking my head. "I don't remember it. There was another picture. With this one."

It leaves just as quickly.

We're both quiet a moment, but I have another question I need to ask.

"When did you take this picture?"

Walker stands up and paces, like he doesn't want to answer.

"When?" I ask softly.

He stops. "On the day of the accident."

"We were together that day?"

His jaw tightens before he answers. "Yeah."

He walks to the bow, and I'm starting to get a knot in my stomach, but I have to know what happened.

"Was I with you when Matt called me to come get him?"

Walker is quiet, like he's thinking about what to say. Then he takes a deep breath and lets it out slowly before he answers.

"Yeah. Sort of."

"What do you mean?"

He comes back over and sits down next to me. "When we brought the boat in, you said you wanted to go back to your house to get something you'd been working on to show me." He pauses. "You said it was important. So you left. Said you'd be quick."

I feel nervous as he talks, knowing that we're getting closer and closer to the accident, and to him having to save me.

"And you were," he says. "You came back, and you were walking down the dock smiling, carrying this big portfolio, and then you stopped to answer your phone. Your whole face changed, and you said something back like you were arguing, and I figured it was Matt."

"He broke up with me the day before that," I say. I tense at the memory of our conversation earlier.

"I know. That's why I thought . . ." He shakes his head.

"What did you think?"

He looks at me for a long moment. "I thought we . . . I don't know. Anyway. You hung up and came over to the boat with your stuff and said you had to go. I didn't ask where or why, but I knew it was him because you were so upset."

"Did you . . ."

He looks at me. "I didn't try to stop you. Wasn't my place."

"And then what? Did I say anything else? Did we . . . I just left?" I'm trying to piece it together in my mind, trying to match up Matt's story with Walker's story.

"You said you'd come back," he says. "And then you left your stuff here."

We sit there quiet for a long time, and I add Matt's story to where Walker's leaves off. I left here to pick him up, put him in my car, and that's how we were on the bridge, in the path of that truck when it lost control. The video footage tells the next part of the story. I see it in my mind, from its shaky beginning to those last words before it cuts out. "There's no way that girl's gonna live."

I look at Walker. "Did you know it was me when you dove in?"

"When I saw him yelling like that, I knew."

I think of him dragging my body onto the boat and doing CPR while Matt panicked. I think of the punch, and the interview, and the way he'd acted toward me after, and now I understand.

"You came to the hospital, didn't you?" I ask. "You brought my camera."

He nods.

"Why?"

"It was important to you."

I try and sort it all out in my head, try to fit everything together so it makes sense. "And then you said yes to the interview?"

Walker exhales slowly. "That reporter told me that you did."

"And then Matt and I showed up together, and . . ." Puzzle pieces are locking into place almost too fast for me to keep up. "You thought . . ."

"That you'd changed your mind."

The boat bumps gently against the dock, and a buoy clinks from somewhere in the inky darkness of the harbor, and Walker and I sit there next to each other, not saying what we both know. That that's the end of the story. The end of our story.

I look at Walker. "I wish I could remember being out on the boat with you that day."

He smiles, but it's sad. "Yeah. Me too."

"I'm sorry," I say.

"Don't be," he answers.

We look at each other, and I think for a second that he might lean in, might bring his lips to mine and kiss me like he didn't get the chance to do before. And I know that if he does, I will bring my hands to his hair, and kiss him back the way I want to now, in this moment.

But he doesn't, and neither do I, and I understand why.

Our moment has passed.

I don't remember him.

I don't remember us, or this.

It's a story I've been told.

That I believe it but don't remember is not enough, and we both know it.

TWENTY-FIVE

I SIT ON my bed the next morning, staring at the blank chalkboard wall, with no idea what comes next.

My mom knocks and tells me there's breakfast downstairs if I'm hungry. I say I'm not and she kisses the top of my head, then leaves. My dad comes in with a piece of mail, sets it on my desk, and asks if I want to "taco 'bout" anything. I laugh for his benefit but say I don't, and he puts his big hand on the back of my neck and squeezes before he goes. Sam comes in to tell me that I can take the day off. I say thank you and ask him to leave. He does.

I feel drained. Heavy with the weight of the things I've both lost and found. And so sad.

Sad that I had this whole relationship with Walker

that I don't remember, that started with this thing we did together. Fixing a boat, of all things. And I'm sad that we missed our chance. But it's not just that.

I'm sad that I'd found my way back to something that I'd loved doing, that I'd given up because somehow it didn't fit into my life. And while I'm happy that I found it again, I don't understand why I felt like I needed to keep it a secret. Or that I felt like Walker needed to be a secret.

I'm sad because out of everything I've found out about myself, these are the things I wish I could take back. Since the accident, I've been trying to be who everyone was telling me I'd been, when that wasn't even me.

But last night felt like it could be me. Sitting there on the boat with Walker really felt like it could be.

Still. He's as much a stranger to me as Matt was, and I can't do the same thing I did with him. I can't just decide to go with the story I've been told, or feel something because I want to, or think I should.

When Walker had dropped me off, I'd told him as much, even though I'd hated the words as I said them, and he'd nodded like he understood, and it felt like the end of something that never was.

But the photo of me from the day we sailed the boat together sits, creased and bent, on my nightstand, and when I look at it, I feel like there had been something. There had been an us. I pick it up and cross the room to my blank chalkboard wall and tuck it into the frame, like a beginning, and then stand back.

That's when I notice the manila envelope my dad had brought in. I don't recognize the address. When I tear the top off and pull out a copy of *Coast Magazine*, my first thought is that it must be another story about the accident and my rescue. There is a note card with it that says, "Your copy, before it hits the stands! Please call for more details when you are feeling up to it. We've been unable to reach you at the number we have." There's a smiley face and a phone number beneath it, and now I'm positive it's a story about that night. These articles have been coming in here and there since I got out of the hospital. I almost just put it in my desk drawer with the others, but then I decide to give it a look. See if it says anything different or new about that night, and me, and Walker. Not that it matters anymore. I know what happened, and I'm done trying to get back the things I've lost. Still, I flip through, looking for whatever little human interest story is there.

But that's not what I find at all.

With the flip of a page, I find something that knocks the breath right out of me. In big, bold letters, at the top of a two-page spread, are the words: *Central Coast Young Artists' Issue: Photo Essay Winner, Teen Category.*

Beneath the words is a shot I recognize and don't. I know

the sunset light in this photo, and the glassy water of the bay beneath it. The hand on the mast.

But those things make up only a tiny piece of what's really there. Of what I'd thought was outside the frame.

In the foreground, there's a large patch of unfinished deck, with two sanding blocks lying off to the side—a work in progress. Walker's silhouette faces the sunset and the open ocean. His broad shoulders look relaxed, as does the way one hand holds on to the mast. The other rests on my shoulder. We stand close, leaving barely a space between us. But we are undeniably together in this moment as we look out over the ocean and horizon and fiery sky spread out in front of us, like endless possibility.

And then there's the title: *The Secret History of Us—a photo essay by Liv Jordan.*

I flip to the next page, and the story begins with a black-and-white photo of *Second Chance*, one that I recognize as having taken years ago, when I'd first gotten my camera and was playing around with different types of film. The next one is of the boat—how it must've been when Walker started working on it and I started taking photos. There are close shots of the weathered sail, the cracked wood. Our hands, working side by side. As the photos of the boat progress, so do the photos of Walker, and of us. The images tell the story of something forgotten brought back to life.

Something lost, but now beautifully found.

And it feels exactly right. I don't have to remember taking those photos to know what they capture. They came from me, from a feeling in me. They are me. And they're Walker. And they're us. And those are the things I know are right.

I need to show him. He needs to see.

I dress quickly, put the magazine into my purse, then head downstairs and out the door. This time I know exactly where I'm going.

I head down to the waterline, where I can walk faster. The sand is wet, and the foamy whitewater comes up to my ankles. It's cold at first—almost bracing. But each time the waves rush up and the water washes over my feet, I notice the cold a little less. I slip into the waves' steady rhythm as I go, and for the first time, I notice that moving like this doesn't hurt. I take a deep breath and fill my lungs to the brim, expecting to feel the protest of my muscles, but there's nothing. Just the absence of pain.

I take another deep breath to be sure, and I try to pay attention because maybe I'm just so used to feeling it by now that it's become a part of me. I stop and look out over the water. Breathe in deep, again and again. And it doesn't hurt anymore. I don't know when, or how, it happened. It wasn't that one breath hurt and the next didn't. But somehow that part of me healed, without me even noticing.

I stand there for a moment, watching the whitewater roll over my feet, and something tumbling around beneath the water catches my eye. I reach for it, then hold the thing up in the sunlight and smile at what I've found.

It's a sand dollar.

When we were little, Sam and I would scour the beach for them, because our dad always told us that if we found a perfect one that still rattled, with no chips or cracks, he'd pay us. He never named a price, but always hinted that the reward would be big. And so we always had an eye out for them on our walks. And there were plenty of them, depending on the tide and the season. But whole sand dollars were rare. I knew they existed because of the bleached-white, dried ones in the Embarcadero shops, but on all our walks we only ever found a few that were still intact. By the time they washed up on the beach, most of them had been tossed and broken by the waves.

I run my thumb over the small white circle in my hand. On the top side that has that little feathery design, it looks nearly perfect. I almost can't believe it. I hold it up to my ear and give it a gentle shake, hoping to hear the quiet rattle of the three little "doves" inside, but there's nothing. I look at it again. Turn it over so I can see the bottom side, which is chipped at the center, just enough for them to have slipped out into the ocean.

I hold in my hand this thing that's been tossed by the

ocean, and broken enough to lose part of itself, but that's still intact, and strong. And I think maybe we're not so different.

I set it down gently on the sand, where it belongs, and then keep going, down to the harbor, to the boat, and Walker, where I belong.

TWENTY-SIX

I DANGLE MY feet over the end of the dock, looking at the empty slip. *Second Chance* is gone, and Walker with it.

This isn't right. He can't be gone. Not now, knowing what I do. Not after I found my way to him a second time. On my own, with choices I made. Just like with taking pictures, and even with Matt. I made the same choices over again without even knowing it. This is me. It's been me. I've spent this whole time trying to find myself when I was here all along. I trust it, finally.

I trust it enough to know the choice I would've made next, because it's the one I make now. I stand up and I walk home, and when I get there, I show my family everything I didn't let them see before.

TWENTY-SEVEN

A FEW DAYS later, I stand in front of the mirror, studying what I see. There, finally, is a reflection I recognize as me—one that I'm happy and proud to show today at the Harbor Festival.

"Liv," my mom calls, "are you ready? We need to get going! The award ceremony is in half an hour."

"Be right there!"

I take one more look in the mirror and realize something is missing, then pick up my Saint Anthony medallion, with its new chain, and fasten the clasp behind my neck. The patron saint of lost things rests on my chest, close to my heart, where he belongs. Now I'm ready.

I go downstairs, and my parents and Sam and I get into

the car and make the short drive to the harbor. I try not to hope too hard that Walker might be back—that he'll get to see this, and I'll get to see him. He's been gone for three days now, and in that time I found out that he'd done something maybe even more incredible for me than saving my life.

When I'd called *Coast Magazine* after I told my parents everything, I found out that my entry had been hand-delivered, the day after the deadline, by a young man who was very insistent that it be accepted. He'd explained my situation, and how hard I'd worked on the project, and how much it had meant to me. And to him.

The secretary had taken it, and the editor had accepted it, and now here I am, about to receive recognition for it at my first mounted photo show.

I scan the faces of the little crowd standing under my tent. The photo editor is there, and a reporter from the local newspaper. Even Dana Whitmore is there for a follow-up interview afterward. Paige stands with my family and gives a little wave. I wave back. We are headed in differ-ent directions, which might have happened before—she's going away to school in the fall, and I'm staying here to work an internship I was offered by the magazine. But her friendship has meant enough to me to hold on to, even as things shift and change. And Jules is there too. She stands behind everyone else, but when I catch her eye, she smiles, and I know, really, she's standing with me.

My heart is full. Almost.

And then all of a sudden it is.

I see Walker, making his way through the festivalgoers, cutting a path straight to where I stand, looking for me, like I've been looking for him. And then our eyes meet.

And we find each other again.

TWENTY-EIGHT

THE MORNING AIR is crisp in a way that carries a hint of fall approaching. An ending and a beginning at the same time. I breathe in deeply as we motor out of the harbor, and I can feel it. Change in the air. Sam has already gone back to school, and Paige left yesterday. I start my internship in a few days, so we've decided to take the boat out, because soon we'll be busy.

Sailing has become our weekend routine, though it's anything but. Every day out here is different. The ocean and the winds, the clouds and the sky. They all make up the ephemeral landscape that we sail through. I try to notice it all, try to capture the details and moments that are here today, but may not be tomorrow. I try to remember the things that are fleeting, but carry something lasting within them. The smell of the salt air, the feel of the wind as it blows tangles into my hair. Walker's hands over mine on the wheel as we cut our own path through the deep blue of the ocean.

The breeze swirls around us, and he brushes a flyaway strand of hair from my face, and then we both lean in—to each other, and everything that's here, now, between us. We come together for a kiss. And here, on the water, when his lips meet mine, I know what I was feeling in that picture that day, and it was this—the feeling of being perfectly who you are, and exactly where you want to be.

I don't know if I'll ever get my memories back, but it doesn't matter because I've stopped chasing them.

I don't think about the past, or before or after.

Instead, I choose now, and the wide-open future that unfolds in front of us, beyond the horizon and the endless sky.

ACKNOWLEDGMENTS

With each book I write, I am more grateful to the amazing people who are there for me every step of the way, from the beginning glimmer of an idea to the finished book sitting on the shelf. I am beyond lucky in life to have you all!

First, I'd like to thank my most favorite people in the world—my family. Thank you for understanding the time it takes to write, and for being there to make the absolute most of the time when I'm not writing. This life is big and beautiful and so much fun because of you!

Next, huge thanks to my agent, Leigh Feldman, who is always there with her invaluable wisdom, guidance, and support.

Of course this book would not be the book it is without the insight and dedication of my incredible editor, Alexandra Cooper. Thank you for your faith in me, and for the energy and heart you put into making each and every page better.

Many thanks to the entire talented team at HarperCollins—Rosemary Brosnan, Alyssa Miele, Kathryn Silsand, Mark Rifkin, Kristen Eckhardt, Bess Braswell, Audrey Diestelkamp, and Olivia Russo. Your kindness and support are beyond amazing. Erin Fitzsimmons, who created this gorgeous, evocative cover, I am forever your fangirl.

To my readers, it is your love for books and reading that always encourages me to continue writing—especially on the hard days. The fact that you're willing to come along with me for a story, or to take the time out of your day and write to me means the world, and I cannot thank you enough for your kind words, support, and enthusiasm. You are the very best!

Of course there would be no story to read if I didn't have the encouragement of friends who are both brilliant and kind: Sarah Ockler, who has talked me off the proverbial edge too many times to count, and on whose living room floor this story began as a set of index cards. Morgan Matson, who always comes to the rescue with much-needed perspective—and Starbucks—when the going gets hard. And my fabulous bacon crew—Carrie Harris, Elana Johnson, Stasia Kehoe, and Gretchen McNeil—I cherish your wit and wisdom more than you could ever know.

My love and gratitude to you all.